Some Boys Have All the Luck . . .

“SKYLAR IN YANKEELAND works the usual Mcdonald charm to good effect . . . He has as much fun with the Yankees as he does with Skylar.”

Boston Globe

“Mcdonald is so smart, terse and witty that he is an outrigh[illegible] to read.”

Peter [illegible]

And praise for Gregory Mcdonald’s previous novel *SKYLAR*

“Endlessly entertaining.”

Publishers Weekly

“Along with delightful characters and a slick plot, Mcdonald provides plenty of fast-moving action.”

Florida Times-Union

“*SKYLAR* ranges from ironic to tittering to out-loud funny.”

Indianapolis Star

“Filled with zest and charm . . . a wickedly humorous whodunit with a style all Mcdonald’s own.”

Booklist

Other Avon Books by
Gregory Mcdonald

CONFESS, FLETCH
FLETCH
FLETCH'S FORTUNE
SKYLAR

Skylar in Yankeeland

GREGORY MCDONALD

AVON BOOKS NEW YORK

AVON BOOKS
A division of
The Hearst Corporation
1350 Avenue of the Americas
New York, New York 10019

Inside cover author photo by Ken Webb
Published by arrangement with the author
Visit our website at **http://www.AvonBooks.com**
Library of Congress Catalog Card Number: 96-18639
ISBN: 0-380-72525-8

Published in hardcover by William Morrow and Company, Inc.; for information address Permissions Department, William Morrow and Company, 1350 Avenue of the Americas, New York, New York 10019.

First Avon Books Printing: January 1998

Printed in the U.S.A.

WCD 10 9 8 7 6 5 4 3 2 1

Dedicated to the three J.J.s, Jamie, Jeremy, and Jason Johnson, with deep appreciation for permitting me in their growing

Skylar in Yankeeland

Chapter 1

Wayne asked his three children, "When is Skylar due to arrive?"

He knew the answer.

"Tomorrow at four," Jon answered. "I'm picking him up at the bus station."

" 'Bus station,' " Calder scoffed. "You had to remind me. Another Dufus. Another flea-scratching, popeyed, twang-talking, Southern farm boy. Racist, I'm sure. 'Ha, y'all!' " Calder grinned like a fool and gestured widely with her arm. Her bracelet jangled. " 'How're y'all doin' this fine day? Me? Why, ah feel just like a mule kickin' high in tall grass!' "

"Dweeb," Ginny called her older sister.

Jon glanced at his father. To his sister Calder, Jon said, "You feel you spent enough time with Dufus to make a judgment?"

"More than enough," Calder answered. "Anything between fifteen and thirty seconds would have been enough."

Lacey, in Bermuda shorts and short-sleeved shirt,

entered the sunroom with a pitcher of lemonade.

As the servants had Thursdays off, her family had the tradition of dining informally Thursday nights. Sometimes, she thought, looking around at her husband and children, perhaps a little too informally. It was the one meal of the week they seldom missed having at home together.

At the round table, her husband, Wayne, sat dressed in a loose tennis shirt and shorts. Since his recent surgery he had regained much of his natural color and weight. But he had not regained his generally good spirits. The three youngsters, their hair still wet from the swimming pool, wore just bikinis, except her son, Jonathan, who, satirically, also wore his Harvard house necktie. They were all end-of-summer tanned. Jon, well over his mononucleosis, had regained his ideal weight and muscle. Calder, to start junior college after Labor Day, sat slouched with one long, slim leg curled around the other. These days Calder was affecting the willowy. At thirteen, Ginny's baby fat had dissolved, leaving her coltish but sleek.

The evening light in the sunroom was beautiful on her children, their clear eyes, their white teeth, their shiny hair, their tanned skin.

"Dufus's proper name," Wayne said, taking his second slice of pizza, "is Anthony Duffy."

"Skylar's not like Dufus." Jon was the only one of the family who knew Skylar. He had spent a short, memorable time with Skylar on the Whitfield Farm in Tennessee earlier in the summer. He had brought Dufus, who worked on the Whitfield Farm, home to Paxton Landing west of Boston for a visit that turned out to be remarkably brief. "Except when he wants to be. As you know, I watched him figure out a difficult situation brilliantly. I mean, Skylar puts on this redneck act, and he has a streak of innocence a mile wide, but, I don't know, as soon as you think you have a handle on him, he flips you over his shoulder."

"We know, dear." Lacey was going around the table pouring lemonade into her husband's and children's glasses. "We all saw your battered face after you spent a week with Skylar."

"Flips you figuratively and literally." Jon smiled. "What I mean is, he may scratch his tick bites in public, but while he's doing it, he is softly whistling 'Eroica.' "

" 'Erotica'?" Ginny wrinkled her nose. "How can you whistle pornography?"

Wayne said, "Please remember Skylar is your cousin." To his wife, he added: "And your nephew."

"Even worse," Calder said. "Do I have to introduce him as a blood relative? I mean, at least we didn't have to account for Dufus."

Wayne said nothing.

"Yes," Jon said. "And Dufus went back to Tennessee after just thirty-six hours of our charming company. We really made him welcome and comfortable, we did."

"Well, hell," Calder said, "how could we make him comfortable? Dufus kept staring at the sky. He thought having more than one airplane visible in the sky at the same time was 'downright dangerous.' He was nervous they were all going to bump into each other and fall on his head or something."

"Who says airplanes won't fall on our heads?" Wayne smiled. "Just because they haven't yet . . ."

Calder said, "So we all should walk around looking up at the sky while tripping over our own feet, Dad?"

"Heads up."

"I don't think so. One or two other things get my attention."

"Boys," Ginny said. "Boys who might fall on you. You wish."

"I expect Skylar is no gentleman," Calder said.

"What's your definition of a gentleman?" her father asked.

"I doubt he knows how to eat a soft-boiled egg," Calder answered, "without making an unseemly mess."

"I see." Wayne stared at his daughter incredulously. "And tell me, Ms., how long does one cook an egg to soft-boil it?"

Calder shrugged. "Eight, ten minutes, I suppose. Something like that."

"I see," Wayne repeated. "Well, that might not soft-boil an egg, but it certainly will make it more portable."

"He knows how to kill a chicken quickly," Jon said. "Like a gentleman."

"How do you kill a chicken quickly like a gentleman?" Ginny asked.

"Twist its neck."

"Uououu."

Sitting at the table, Lacey said, "I'm sure that soon after Skylar's term begins at the Knightsbridge School of Music next week, and he is living in the room in Boston Jon has arranged for him, Skylar will make his own friends."

"And so we won't have to see him very much?" Calder asked happily.

"This will be his home away from home," Lacey pronounced. "Your father and Skylar's father are brothers. As your father so pointedly insists upon reminding us. Which is why he brought up the topic of Skylar's arrival at this juncture."

The look of mutual curiosity, with which the children were well familiar, passed between husband and wife.

"Should we get some fleas and ticks and scatter them around the yard to make him feel at home?" Ginny asked. "How about placing a few cow flops artfully on the lawn? We could start a trend. *New England Taste* might feature Paxton Landing again."

"We should import some copperhead and cottonmouth snakes, too," Jon said. "Rattlers. Wolves, coyotes. And don't forget wrapadangs."

"What's a wrapadang?" Ginny asked.

"Oh, you never want to come across a wrapadang," Jon warned her.

"I don't think it's fair for you to be prejudiced against the South," Wayne said. "Or Southerners. Your father is a Southerner. Are you prejudiced against me? Especially since Calder, with prejudice, just hypothesized Skylar is a racist. You don't know that he is. Do you consider me a racist?"

" 'Hypothesized'?" Ginny frowned. "I wonder if Louise Uglythorpe can spell that one."

"Why did you leave the South?" Calder asked her father.

"There weren't many opportunities there, at that time. When I left."

"You've never been back," Lacey said.

"No," Wayne said. "I haven't."

Ginny asked Jon, "What's Skylar really like?"

"Well, he's nine feet tall, has two heads, feet that are a meter long—"

"Good," Ginny said. "He won't need to borrow our skis."

Jon laughed. "I doubt you'll ever see Skylar Whitfield on skis. That boy slows down walkin' on wet grass."

"Good!" Calder said. "We won't have to invite him for Christmas in Vail."

"Actually, he can be quite charming," Jon said. "At least the ladies seem to like him. Rather too much, I'd say. And he can play the trumpet like you've never heard it played before."

"Sure," Calder said. "But I've already heard 'When the Saints Go Marching In.' "

Lacey said, "I surely hope young Skylar does not think our annual Labor Day formal party Saturday is in his honor."

"Aunt Monica and Uncle Dan gave me a big welcoming party."

"Never," said Lacey, "would I dare imitate Southern manners. Whatever they are."

"They are difficult to comprehend," Jon muttered. "In the South, you can hit someone upside the head, but you're supposed to do so only in a kindly manner, and with the best of intentions."

"Closer to my definition of a gentleman," Wayne said.

His wife said: "Of course."

"What I'm trying to say," Wayne said, "is that there is no reason to be prejudiced against your cousin Skylar. You don't even know him."

"Are you saying we have to wait until after we know Skylar to be prejudiced against him?" Calder asked.

"But, Wayne," Lacey said, "you've ignored your nephew all his life."

"Guilty as charged," Wayne admitted. "My

brother's family hasn't been much of a factor in our lives."

"I'm not prejudiced against him." Ginny took her fifth piece of pizza. "I liked Dufus. He was funny. Of course, I didn't understand much of what he said."

"That may be all for the best," Calder said. "I understood a bit of what he said."

Lacey asked, "Wayne, tomorrow will you stop by the bank, please, and pick up my tiara rig for the party?"

"Not that old thing again." Calder smiled.

"Sure," Wayne said.

"I'm wearing that rather regal gown I ordered in London in June."

"It arrived?" Calder asked.

"Last week."

"You never showed us," Calder complained.

"Show us after supper?" Ginny asked.

"If you ever stop eating," her mother said.

Wayne said to his son, "The arrival of a gown is of more interest than the arrival of a blood relative."

"I suppose we'll have to have Alex Broadbent to the party." Lacey sighed. "The Broadbent flotilla."

"Unavoidable," Wayne said, "as long as he lives in our boathouse."

Lacey said, "His entourage are like vermin."

Wayne said, "I think mostly he feeds his entourage appetizers provided by others."

Calder said, "Alex is brilliant. He interests people. Everybody reads his column in *The Star*."

"Then why," Lacey asked patiently, "do people have to see him? Him and his utterly boring wife? Especially when people are coming here supposedly to see us, not them? I rather wish we'd leased the boathouse to someone far less interesting. A mass murderer or something. Well, maybe he'll arrive late, as usual."

Wayne chuckled. "He'll still arrive like the Seventh Fleet."

"He'll apologize to me, saying he just can't get rid of people."

Ginny said, "He can't."

Wayne stood up from the round table and stretched his arms over his head, something he never would do with servants in the house. "I, for one, look forward to meeting my nephew. It should be amusing."

"Skylar is amusing, all right," Jon said. "About as amusing as a cricket in your shorts."

"No. I don't want you doing that," Jonesy said.

"Doing what?"

"What you're doing with your hand."

"Which hand?"

Jonesy grabbed Jon's hand and twisted his wrist, suddenly and hard.

Not expecting such force, Jon said, "Ow. Oh. That hand." His other hand rubbed his hurt wrist. "What was I doing so bad?"

"You were rubbing inside my hipbone with your thumb."

"Oh. You didn't like that?"

"No.

"Sorry."

Shortly after lunch Friday they lay naked on Jon's single bed in Suite A-15 in Harvard's Calder House.

For a moment, they stopped making love to each other.

"Gee," Jon said.

"Now, don't lose it."

"Lose what?"

"Your enthusiasm."

"I, uh—"

Jonesy slapped his face, just hard enough to make it sting.

Typically during the school year they met Friday afternoons, either in Jon's room, or Jonesy's, across the hall, and made love to each other. Jonesy had said it helped relieve their weekends of tension.

During holidays they met where and when they could.

Thursday night Jon had called Jonesy asking that they meet earlier than usual Friday, since he had to meet his cousin at four. As the term had not yet started, Calder House was not yet open to students. Jon said his excuse for their going to his suite was that he had to buy books at the Harvard Coop he might as well leave in his suite.

"Come on." Jonesy rolled on top of him. "Just do as I say."

Jon rolled on top of Jonesy.

Jonesy flipped Jon off the bed onto his back on the floor.

"Hey!" On the floor, Jon sat up on his elbows.

Jonesy's fingers played with the hair of his head. "Are you going to be a good boy now?"

"I don't know."

"Sure you are."

"When do we get to do as I say?"

"Never," Jonesy answered. "Now come on back up here."

Jon climbed back onto the bed. And onto Jonesy.

"Now just do as I say," Jonesy said. "No more. No less."

* * *

"One thing I'll say for you, Jon. You're cool."

"I have a choice?"

There was sweat on Jonesy's upper lip and neck.

Jon was cool.

"Aren't you happy?" Jonesy asked.

"Don't you think it might be better, for both of us," Jon asked, "if you allow me to contribute something to the sex act besides—above and beyond—the purely mechanical?"

"You mean, if I let you do more of what you want to do?"

"Yeah." Jon stuck his thumb between two of his ribs, which somehow had become bruised. "Like that."

"God." Jonesy stood up from the bed and went to the desk chair where her underpants and bra and skirt and shirt were. "Who knows what that might be?"

"What are you doing?"

"Getting dressed."

"It's only two-thirty. Aren't you going to the bus station with me?"

"To pick up your guitar-pickin' cousin?"

"Trumpet. Skylar plays the trumpet."

"Whatever. Is playing a trumpet much of an accomplishment?" Jonesy dropped Jon's pressed shorts onto the floor. "I've got something to do."

"What?"

"Mister Sensitive. As if I want to go to a bus station. As if I can hardly wait to say 'Howdy-do' and shake hands with some lumpy boy who thinks in terms of hens and roosters and cows and bulls. I might catch poison ivy from him."

"Skylar's not lumpy."

"I'll meet him tonight, dinner at Paxton Landing." She swung her leather handbag over her shoulder. "I can hardly wait."

Still on his mattress, Jon listened to Jonesy cross the living room, leave the suite, and go down the stone stairs.

He guessed she was going to see her psychiatrist. Isn't that where everybody went, all the time?

And the psychiatrist would assure Jonesy that her version of events, including lovemaking, was correct.

Isn't that why people went to psychiatrists?

Chapter 2

"Ha, Jon Than! How're ya doin'?"

"Ha, Skylar! You all right?"

The cousins shook hands.

Four-thirty Friday afternoon before the Labor Day weekend the bus terminal was jammed with diverse people going in diverse directions at diverse speeds.

"Miss my dog," Skylar said.

"Your 'dawg.' And your horse, and your homemade pickup truck, and your parents, and Dufus . . . ?" Jon stopped. He wanted to say, And you miss Tandy McJane. . . . Since leaving the farm weeks before, Jon had thought a lot about Tandy McJane and Skylar, who had grown up together, and not as brother and sister.

"And my gun." Skylar looked around the terminal. "Don't I see some people 'round here that need shootin' real bad?"

"Yes, you do."

"What're those weird-lookin' men doin' sittin' on that bench against the wall? They're not goin' anywhere. They haven't got any luggage. Nobody would want 'em to visit anyway."

"They're lookin' for chickens to pluck."

"What does that mean? What's a chicken?"

"You are."

"Beg pardon, cousin?"

"They're looking for runaway kids, male and female, getting off the buses they can turn to drugs and prostitution."

"You serious? They're allowed to sit there and do that?"

"It's a free country. A land of opportunity. Free enterprise. Haven't you heard?"

"Well . . ." Skylar had dropped his daddy's big suitcase on the floor beside him to shake Jon's hand. He still held his trumpet case in his other hand. "I got my horn, anyway."

"Hey, Skylar!" A man passing them slapped Skylar on the shoulder. "Good luck to you, son!"

Jon frowned.

A teenaged girl, a chicken probably about to be plucked, batted her false eyelashes and said, "I'll see you around, Skylar."

Jon asked, "What's this about? How come these people know you?"

"Well, sir, it was a long trip, surely too far for anyone to go. Somewhere north of Washington, D.C., someone asked me if I could play this thing—" Again, Skylar held up the trumpet case.

An older woman stopped. She beamed into Skylar's face.

She said, "You sure do play that horn real purty, Skylar."

"Thank you, ma'am."

"So you gave a concert on the bus?"

"Prolly why the bus is a little late. The driver took a likin' for that ditty I call 'Sarah Serendipity'? Anyway, sorry to keep you waitin'."

"I don't think I know that one."

"You want me to play it for you now?"

"Not here, Skylar." An older couple stopped to wish Skylar luck. They invited him to their coffee shop in Dorchester to try her Boston cream pie. "Skylar, you already know more people in Boston than I do, and I've lived here all my life."

Skylar shrugged. "I never met a stranger."

"Well"—Jon clapped Skylar on the shoulder—"you're about to." Jon picked up the big suitcase. "You're about to meet a lot of strangers."

Following Jon across the terminal, Skylar said, "Did you hear I won a demolition derby?"

"No. Somehow news of that didn't get to me."

"Well, I did. After Dufus came home from visiting you all, he started putting this old car together. Mrs. Duffy sponsored it. So we painted THE HOLLER all over the car real big and pretty to advertise her place of business."

"That splendid Greendowns County cultural and social institution?"

"Yeah. Her roadhouse. We won us two hundred and fifty dollars."

"How much did putting the car together cost, parts and labor?"

"Oh, maybe a thousand."

"The South Shall Rise Again," Jon said.

"I drove in the derby," Skylar said. "Dufus was too nervous about the car catchin' on fire. He said he doubted his whole belly would fit through the car window."

"Good. You can drive home." Jon handed Skylar the car keys.

"Hold on a minute there, Jon Than."

Jon stood in traffic. "What's the matter?"

"You're crossing this big old road right in the middle, cars goin' every which way." Skylar looked to the end of the block. "Aren't there stop signs somewhere in this town?"

"It's called jaywalking." Jon continued to lug the suitcase across traffic. He yelled over his shoulder: "It's our number one sport here in Boston. More popular than baseball, football, and ice hockey combined."

"Whoa!" Following Jon, Skylar stopped in the road and held up his hand for a car to stop. It did not stop. Blaring its horn, it swerved around him.

"Come on!" Jon yelled at him. "You're giving them too much chance to hit you."

Almost running into the back of a moving car, Skylar dashed across the road.

"Lordy, Lordy, Jon Than! Haven't these folks got any manners? Couldn't they see you were carryin' my daddy's big suitcase?" Jon placed the suitcase on the backseat of a small convertible parked next to a No Parking sign. "What kind of vehicle is that?"

"A BMW."

"Who'd let you borrow a fancy chariot like that?"

"You're sweating, Skylar."

"Yeah. Well. It ain't the heat. It's this jaybirdin' sport you're tryin' to coach me on. At least in the demolition derby I had some reinforced steel around me. Here all I got are two feet and wobbly knees."

"Hey, you little shits!" A huge man stormed across the sidewalk at them from a parking lot. "You see that sign?"

"Is he talkin' to you that way, Jon Than?"

"Ignore him."

"He weighs a good two-sixty, Jon Than."

"You blocked my entrance!" The man kicked a fender of the car. "You rich little bastards!"

"Well, my cousin may have a rich daddy," Skylar drawled, "but, me, I'm just a farm boy from Greendowns County, Tennessee."

"Your lot was full." Jon sat on the passenger seat of the car and closed the door.

Skylar stood directly in front of the man. "I'm real sorry if my cousin caused you any inconvenience, mister. I'm sure he wasn't tryin' to do you any purposeful harm."

"What?"

"How can we make it up to you?"

"What?" The man squinted into Skylar's face. "Gimme twenty bucks."

The man held out his hand.

Skylar shook it.

"Skylar!"

Skylar said, "Mister, you sure look like you've got some Cullin blood in you."

"What're you talkin' about? What do you mean, 'Cullin blood'?"

"By any chance you any kin to the Cullin family in Greendowns County, Tennessee?"

"What are you, crazy?"

"You have the same cast to your eyes. Exact same squint. I recognize it. The Cullins run to fat, too."

"My grandmother," the big man said. "Her maiden name was Collins."

"That's right," Skylar said. "Names in the South are apt to get spelled any which way. Cullin, Collins, all the same. I'm right pleased to make your acquaintance."

"You know my grandmother's family?"

"I surely do. Terry Cullin ran for commissioner of roads, last election. We voted for him."

"Did he win?"

"No, sir, he didn't. We voted for him, but not enough times, I guess."

"Well, I'll be damned. You know some of my family I don't even know about. Sure, my grandmother came from somewhere down there, where you're from. You live anywhere near Arkansas?"

"Sure do. We slip back and forth all the time. Why, they're a fine family, the Cullins are. Without the Cullin family, we couldn't keep both our grocery stores runnin'."

"Skylar!" Jon growled. "Get in the damned car!"

"My cousin's impatient," Skylar said. "I do apologize for him."

"Road commissioner. I'll be damned." The man closed the driver's door after Skylar got behind the wheel. "You come back and talk to me sometime, willya, kid?"

"Well, sir, I'll sure try. I surely will."

"I own this parking lot here."

"Why, that's just fine. Tyler Cullin has a body shop out beyond Crosstrees."

"Would he be some sort of a cousin of mine?"

"I expect he would. Same shape to his eyes. It's that squint that gives you away. Guess we've got to go now, before my cousin has an accident."

"Skylar . . ."

"I'll tell my kids I met someone who knows some of my family. Wait a minute. I'll hold the traffic for you."

The big man walked into the street. For him, the cars made a wide path.

Skylar slid the convertible into a lane perfectly empty of traffic. Proceeding slowly, he waved back at the man.

Jon stared at his cousin. "Skylar . . . how did you do that? Did you make all that up?"

"No, sir, I did not. Whoa!" Skylar braked sharply. "Missed that one. Was that a taxi? Well, Jon Than, when you're brought up studying cows and bulls and horses and dogs, and people, you learn to recognize similarities in the lineage. That man had Cullin eyes as sure as God made turnips. Even squinted the same."

"You're talking about breeding. My God, you're talking about breeding."

"Is that a Baptist church over there?"

"It used to be a church. It's an art film house."

"The Cullins have very distinctive eyes. I'd recognize a Cullin anywhere. Didn't you notice?"

"There really is a Cullin family in Greendowns County?"

"Sure. Phew! What's that crazy road doin' comin' in there at that angle!"

"Stop braking. You're snapping my neck."

"That church over there. Is it Baptist?"

"Now it's a store. Sells electronics."

"Now if you ever see another Cullin, you'll recognize him, right? Just remember there isn't a one of them yet who hasn't run to fat, exceptin' Addy. She didn't bloom until after she was comfortably married. They used to call her 'poor Addy' before she met up with Thirlbert—Love a duck! That truck came over on me as if we weren't here at all!"

"Turn right at the light."

"No, sir, I won't. I'm stoppin' right here."

"You can't stop here, Skylar. We're in the middle of traffic."

"I didn't hear you say anything about the possibility of my winning two hundred and fifty dollars for driving through this stretch of Boston, now, did I?"

"Skylar, at least pull over to the side."

"They won't let me. I've only got this far without wreckin' 'cause I'm a God-fearin' Baptist."

"Goddamn it, Skylar!"

Jon got out and ran around the back of the car and opened the driver's door.

"Move over!"

Skylar's eyes were closed. Sweat poured down his face.

Ignoring the horns blasting them, patiently Skylar said, "Jon Than? That makes it twice now, on this short ride, you've taken the Lord's name in vain."

"Skylar, you'd drive anyone either to drink or to pray or both. Move over, or, goddamn it, I'll kick your butt from here to . . ."

Skylar looked up at his cousin. "Kingdom Come?"

"To goddamn Greendowns County!"

Lifting himself over the console to the passenger seat, Skylar muttered, "I'm beginin' to think there's not all that much difference between Kingdom Come and Greendowns County, I am. Give me my druthers at this minute, I'd choose either over this here Boston of yours."

Chapter 3

Not standing up from his computer console at Paxton Landing, Wayne Whitfield simply looked up when his son and Skylar entered his study. He looked at Skylar, and said, "Mr. Lowenstein."

"No, Dad."

The two young men stood in front of Wayne Whitfield's large, ornate desk.

" 'Mr. Lowenstein'?" Skylar asked. "Well, sir, I'd say you're not too good at recognizing family. I'm your nephew, Skylar."

Wayne said, "I thought you'd say something like that."

"You look a bit like my daddy," Skylar said. "How come you talk like a Yankee?"

"I've been here a while." Studying his nephew as he might the figures on his computer screen, Wayne said, "Cutoff blue jeans and a T-shirt that I suspect once was more white than its present dingy gray."

"I spent the night on a bus."

"We've got to do something about his clothes, Jonathan. We're dressing for dinner tonight. I don't suppose you have black tie, do you, Skylar?"

"Got a yellow tie."

"Mr. Lowenstein is a very fine tailor. For us, he'll whip up proper clothes for you in no time. Why don't you bring Skylar back to town, Jonathan, give Mr. Lowenstein a chance at him?"

"Not appropriate, Dad. Skylar can borrow clothes of mine."

"I got a pair a jeans and a T-shirt I ain't even worn yet, if that's what you all are worried about."

"We have an ambassador and his wife coming to dinner, Skylar. You see, in a way, when you have a foreign ambassador and his wife for dinner, well, we're sort of representing this country. . . ."

"Nothing's more American than blue jeans and T-shirts," Skylar said.

"Nice," Wayne Whitfield said. "You're not here five minutes and we're arguing about clothes."

"I noticed that," Skylar said. "Why, Uncle Wayne, I thought you'd give me a big howdy-do-how's-your-folks?"

"Howdy. How's your folks?"

"Aren't you interested in the farm, at all?"

"How's the farm?"

"The tobacco's lookin' real good."

"You still growing tobacco?"

"Some folks have shifted to cotton. But that takes equipment we can't afford, for the little we can grow."

Wayne sighed. "Congratulations on winning that scholarship to Knightsbridge, Skylar."

"Thank you, sir."

"I look forward to hearing your music," Wayne mumbled.

Jon smiled at his father. "He gave a concert on the bus."

"Has your mother met Skylar yet? Your sisters?"

"No."

Skylar said, "No one seemed to be here when we arrived, 'cept some man in uniform packin' a pistol who wrote our names down on a clipboard."

"Security," Wayne said. "I brought your mother's tiara home from the bank."

"I know," Jon said. "I explained to Skylar I don't usually have to sign in and out of my own home."

"Why, your house is older than our house," Skylar said. "And I thought you were rich folks."

Father and son exchanged glances.

Wayne said, "Paxton Landing was a tavern even before the American Revolution, Skylar."

"You mean a roadhouse?"

"Of a sort. An inn," Wayne said. "For people traveling on the river."

"You got a lot of sheds jammed all together in a small space, Uncle. One catches afire, and you've lost 'em all."

"Sheds? Oh, the guesthouse, the pool house—"

"And a car house with seven different doors."

"Yes."

"That pasture goin' down to the river," Skylar said. "You could have at least a few goats on that."

"Yes. I suppose we could."

"I mean, with what the goats could bring in, you could at least get rid of some of those big stones on your driveway, in a few years."

"That's a cobblestone driveway," Wayne said. "Dates from the late eighteenth century."

"Time it got tore up," Skylar said. "Wouldn't you say?"

Uncle and nephew continued to look at each other.

Wayne asked his son, "He is kidding, isn't he?"

Jon shrugged. "You tell me."

Wayne turned back to his computer. "Dinner at eight. Appetizers on the terrace at seven. Black tie. Copies of the bios of dinner guests are in your room. Nice meeting you, Skylar."

"You must meet lots of people in your business, Uncle."

"I do."

"I can tell," Skylar said.

"Why do you say that?"

"You make so little of it when you do meet someone."

"You're getting quite a lot of attention from the ambassador," Jonesy said to Skylar at dinner. "Rather too much attention, I'd say."

His aunt Lacey sat at the head of the table, to his right.

Jonesy sat to his left.

The ambassador sat across from him.

Jon had taken Skylar to his mother's bedroom, where he met his aunt Lacey, his cousins Calder and Ginny, and Jonesy.

The women were admiring a mostly diamond tiara, eardrops, necklace, and bracelet. They said hello to Skylar.

Ginny wanted to try on the tiara, Calder, the necklace.

Skylar paid about as much attention to the gems as the women paid to him.

Still speaking softly at the dinner table, Jonesy said,

"I expect the ambassador has never heard anyone talk the way you do."

"He's just bein' polite, I reckon," Skylar said. "Isn't that an ambassador's job? To be polite?"

"Not to you," Jonesy said.

The ambassador had shown interest in Skylar's music.

Skylar asked the ambassador about musical instruments native to his country.

At home, in his own country, the ambassador had assembled the biggest and best collection of native drums.

For Skylar, he described and explained almost every drum in the collection.

"I expect there are people here trying to do business with the ambassador," Jonesy said.

"Do business? Like what kind of business?"

"Sell his country goods and services."

"Who here is trying to sell the ambassador on goods and services?"

"Your uncle Wayne, for one."

"I thought we were representing America, or some such thing."

"You've been usurping the conversation," Jonesy said. "It's just the way you talk."

"Could it be the way I listen?"

After leaving his suitcase in Jon's room, Skylar and Jon had horsed around in the swimming pool. Ginny, making a quick change in the pool house, joined their splash party.

Jonesy also had changed into a swimsuit. But she did not go into the pool.

Behind dark glasses she sat under an umbrella and watched the three Whitfields wrestling with each other in the water.

Arms around his neck, Ginny rode Skylar's back while Jon pounded his stomach, then held his head under water. Skylar tackled Jon under water and threatened to hold him down. The two male cousins threw the wriggling Ginny back and forth through the water like a giant beanbag.

After watching awhile, Jonesy left the pool area.

"Tell me," Jonesy asked Skylar at dinner, "did Jon have to tie your tie for you?"

"He taught me how." He tugged at the two ends of his bow tie and beamed at her. "Did I do a good job of it, finally?"

"No."

". . . gave a concert on the bus." Jon's voice fell into a momentary silence at the table.

"Ah!" the ambassador said. "I'm sure the people appreciated that, very much."

"In the terminal in Boston Skylar was treated almost as a celebrity," Jon said.

Turning his head to look at Jon down the table, the ambassador said, "I have invited your cousin to my country. I think our native music would interest him very much. He could see my collection of drums."

"Skylar's never met a stranger." Jon laughed. "I parked my car illegally outside the terminal and when we came out there was this irate parking-lot attendant who swore at us and kicked my car. In about thirty seconds Skylar had woven this tale for him about how this jerk must have relatives in Tennessee, Skylar insisted he recognized a family resemblance, one ran a body shop, another even might have been road commissioner, and this jerk fell for it, he got all excited, believed every word, believed Skylar knew his grandmother's family or something, and all the time Skylar's actually calling him and his whole family fat slobs who squint."

Laughing, the ambassador said, "I foresee a future in diplomacy for young Skylar."

Wayne, unsmiling, studied his nephew.

Jon said, "It was like seeing a big hornet get all wrapped up in a spider's web. He was even flapping his arms like wings in excitement because he believed Skylar knew some of his long-lost family. He invited Skylar to come back and visit him. He even stopped traffic to let us out of where we were illegally parked!"

"How amusing," Uncle Vance Calder said. "Skylar foiled a parking-lot attendant."

Sitting back, arms folded across his chest, Skylar said, "Boston sure is a pretty city. And Bostonians must be the best drivers in the whole world! Somehow they keep missin' each other. I don't see how they do it, no way."

"There isn't as much traffic in Boston as it appears," Judge Ferris said. "Actually, there are only five or six cars in the whole city. It's just that the streets are so narrow and twisty, and they're all one-way, and because there is nowhere to park, you see, the traffic you think is heavy is really . . ." Pausing, he looked up from under heavy eyebrows at Skylar.

"Well, I'll be a naked bareback rider on a flea-infested horse!" Skylar exclaimed. "They're all the same five or six cars just goin' around and around!" The judge laughed delightedly. "Is that how they do it?" Skylar asked. "They're so used to drivin' against each other . . ."

"That's it!" The judge raised his fork in the air. "They know each other's terrible driving habits!"

"That's how they keep barely missin' each other," Skylar marveled. "I did wonder."

"At home," Jon said, "Skylar won a demolition derby. But he wouldn't drive in Boston."

Calder said, "Oh, my God."

Skylar said, "I need to study up on those other five or six other drivers before I try it again."

"What's this whatever-it-is derby?" the ambassador asked.

"A bunch of harebrained idiots fix up wrecks of old cars and smash them into each other. Last car still able to move wins." Calder sniffed. "It doesn't happen much around here, I'm glad to say."

"Just on Route Six," Dotty Palmer said. "Every Friday and Sunday night, June to September."

"No, ma'am," Skylar said. "In a real demolition derby you can't go more than three minutes without crashin' into another car."

"As I said: exactly like Route Six."

"Sounds like fun," the ambassador said. "I have a wreck of an old car. A three-year-old Mercedes."

Dr. Danforth asked Skylar, "And exactly how does one win a demolition derby?"

"Well, sir, I learned from studyin' a man all my life named Mr. Newton. He usually wins. He just didn't happen to be drivin' in the derby I won. What you do is hunker down. Hunker down," Skylar repeated. "When you have to hit a car, you just sneak out and tap it, then go try and hide again. Let all the other drivers destroy each other. Then, when they're all wrecked, your car is still in pretty good shape, you see? Then you drive out and finish wreckin' the one or two cars that can still move!"

Skylar smiled around the table, at the flushed

Jonesy, the pale Calder, the studious Uncle Wayne, grinning Jon, gaping Aunt Lacey.

"That does sound like fun," the judge said. "May I borrow your Mercedes, Mr. Ambassador?"

Elbows on the table, Calder put her face in her hands. Beside her, Tom Palmer, Jr., took one of her hands away from her face and held it.

They seemed embarrassed at witnessing someone else's tragedy.

"Just like diplomacy!" the ambassador marveled. "Hunker and tap, hunker and tap, then, wreck 'em!"

"Yes, sir," Skylar said, "you got it exactly right."

The ambassador said, "Well, I'll be a flea on a naked horse!"

After dinner, alone, Skylar went onto the terrace.

Moonlight reflected from the river. Down to Skylar's right, electric lights shone from a structure either very near or on the river.

Skylar heard faintly a strange music. It appeared to be a banjo backed by an acoustic guitar backed by pizzicato violin, cello, and bass. He could not hear it well enough to follow it.

He turned his back to the river and sat on the wide, stone balustrade.

He had had the emotions of leaving home, had been more awake than asleep all night on the bus, and had met all these people here: the ambassador and his wife; Judge Ferris, a widower; Dr. and Mrs. Danforth; Vance Calder, Jon's uncle, and his fifth wife; his own uncle, Wayne Whitfield, about whom Skylar had always been curious and whom he had expected to greet with a hug, as he would his own father, or at least a handshake, but who had greeted him rather as one more problem, one more thing to be solved, by a busy man; his aunt Lacey, who hadn't even asked him if he was hungry, or thirsty, or tired; Calder and her boyfriend, Tom Palmer, both of whom seemed ashamed of him; Ginny, who, being prepubescent, seemingly remained open, free of problems; Jonesy, whose every line seemed critical of him, but who at least looked at him and spoke to him.

On the terrace of Paxton Landing on this warm August night, wearing a jacket, Skylar shivered.

He wondered if it would be understood, accepted as polite, if he sneaked off to bed.

He wondered what was considered polite in this rich land devoid of animals, where clothes and gems were more admired than the people wearing them.

One of the French doors opened.

Jonesy crossed the terrace to him. She stood between his knees. "Hi."

"Hi."

" 'Ha,' " she said. "You said, 'Ha.' "

"These folks have a dog, or a cat, or a horse, or anything?"

She placed her hips against the balustrade between his legs. "You want to ride a horse?"

"I wouldn't mind."

"I don't know anyone like you," Jonesy said.

"I figured that."

"I mean, I bet you spend all day every day doing physical things, things with your body."

"Doesn't everyone?"

"No. Every night, too?"

Twisting his neck, Skylar looked at the drop-off from the balustrade behind him. It was about four meters.

"Your real name is Joan," he said.

"That's right. And your name is Skylar. And you're real."

"Right," Skylar said. "Real poor. Real dumb."

"Real sexy."

"Who says that?"

"I do."

"Aren't you supposed to be my cousin's girlfriend?"

"We're friends," she said. "I'm a girl."

"I noticed that." Skylar thought of Tandy McJane. Deeply, he had been thinking of her anyway.

Gripping the balustrade with his fingers outside his legs, he swung his left leg over Jonesy's head and jumped off the balustrade as he might a horse.

Jonesy's eyes popped wide.

"Well." Arms folded across his chest, he leaned his lower back against the balustrade. "Guess I better go call my parents. Tell 'em I arrived safely. Met my uncle and aunt and cousins. Made new friends."

Jonesy turned. This time she pressed her hips against his left leg. "Tell me, Skylar, what did you think of your aunt's baubles?"

Skylar blushed. "What do you mean, her baubles?"

"Her tiara, necklace . . ."

"Oh. Her gembobs. I'd call 'em glittery, I guess. Why do they need their own armed guard?"

"Skylar. They're appraised for something more than five million dollars."

"Five million!"

"Shh."

"You mean, those polished bottom-of-the-creek stones are worth more than everything in Greendowns County except the minister's daughter?"

Jonesy's eyes remained in his.

"Well, I'll be—" Skylar said.

"See?" Jonesy placed her fingertips on Skylar's leg.

"Sure," Skylar said. "I can see why my cousins feel they don't need to mess with goats."

Weary of the sound of too many stringed instruments being plucked in his huge living room, Alex Broadbent slipped through the door onto the deck of the boathouse. The deck was raised well above the surface of the river.

On the river many lights reflected from the main house. The Labor Day weekend parties of the family Whitfield had begun.

Sipping his iced coffee, Alex smiled at the arrogance of the very rich. The one weekend of the year most friends and business associates of the Whitfields preferred to spend at their summer homes, at the seaside or in the mountains, maybe even closing their houses for the season, saying good-bye for now to their summer sets of friends, the Whitfields demanded their presence at Paxton Landing for their annual, too formal bash.

The Whitfields demanded.

And the people came.

And, before leaving, invariably the guests said, "Thank you so much for inviting us."

Some of the guests probably meant it.

Is it that the very rich can afford to be oblivious to their own stupidity, inconsiderateness?

Or do the very rich oblige others to suffer their intentional stupidity as a practice in power?

Alex thought there might be a column to write based on these two questions. He would have to observe and think more on the topic.

Chapter 4

"Jon Than?"

"Moan."

"Can you please tell me why there are police cars in the driveway?"

Returning from the bathroom, Skylar was bathed in the sunlight coming through the casement window.

Still in his bed, Jon said, "Because you're standing naked in front of a window? I'd ask where you were brought up, except I know."

Having dried his hair, Skylar put the towel around his waist. "Really. Why would the police be here?"

"I don't know. Who cares?"

"Something wrong with you?"

"A little too much wine last night."

"That why you talked so much about me at dinner?"

"Guess so. Sorry. I was bored."

"If I told my friends and family in Greendowns County about how you behaved down there, they wouldn't like you, either. Remember that night in the quarry?"

"Oh, shut up."

"That's all I'm sayin'."

"What?"

"Shut up."

"Why are the cops here?" Jon led Skylar into the dining room and instantly began loading a plate from the buffet.

At the table, with Tom Palmer, Jr., and Ginny, Calder yawned. "Mama's rocks got heisted, or some such thing."

"Oh. I thought you and Tom were playing in the club's golf tournament this morning. Want some sausage, Skylar?"

"We are," Calder said. "First the police had to interview us. We are now free to go. What a bore. The 'rents are still with the fuzz."

"So why haven't you left?" Jon asked.

Calder smiled at Obadiah, the butler. He was removing used plates from the two ends of the table.

"Rocks?" Skylar sat at the table across from Jon. "Your mama has a rock garden?"

"Sure," said Calder. "All gardens in New England are rock gardens. Rocks are what we grow best."

"Why would the police care about what happens to your mama's rocks?" Skylar tasted his scrambled eggs.

Calder stretched. "Why indeed?"

Wayne entered. At the sideboard he poured himself a cup of coffee.

Obadiah placed a soft-boiled egg in a cup on Skylar's plate.

Skylar looked up at the butler. "I already have an egg, thank you, sir."

Obadiah did not remove the soft-boiled egg.

Watching from the sideboard, Wayne glanced at Calder. "I see."

"Any clues?" Tom Palmer asked.

Wayne sat at his end of the table. "Not that I know of. The police are questioning everybody. Searching the servants' rooms."

"Where was the guard who was supposed to be watching the jewelry?" Jon asked.

"He says he spent the entire night sitting within five meters of the safe in the study. From the moment I checked the safe before I went to bed." Wayne turned the newspaper next to his plate to scan the bottom of the front page. "My, my. That plan for a new skyscraper on Broad Street seems to be going forward. He insists he did not fall asleep. He did not leave the room for a minute."

"Not even to pee?" Ginny asked.

Her father corrected her. "Not even to relieve himself."

Skylar stared at his uncle. "Are you trying to tell me Aunt Lacey's jewelry was stolen during the night?"

"I'm not trying to tell you anything, Skylar. But, yes, some of your aunt Lacey's jewelry has gone missing during the night."

"The jewelry I saw last night in her bedroom?"

"What jewelry did you see last night?"

"A headpiece, a neckpiece, a wristpiece—"

"And two earpieces," Calder said. "Didn't you see the nosepiece?"

"Wow."

Jon asked, "So how did you discover it's missing?"

"The insecurity guard, as we may now speak of him, called me on the house phone at dawn. The security light below the safe behind my desk had gone off. Of course he thought it was just a blown fuse or something."

"Hell," Tom Palmer scoffed. "The jerk slept all night, woke up at dawn, and discovered the safe had been broken into."

"It hadn't been broken into," Wayne said. "When I came downstairs the safe doors were closed and locked. The police tell me there is no evidence of force used. But that section of the safe was empty."

"He closed the door himself," Tom said.

"Come on," Calder said. "He had all night to open the safe and steal the jewelry himself. And transport it wherever he wanted. Right now it's probably being chopped into little pieces in Madagascar."

Wayne turned to the newspaper's Sports section. "The police are holding him for further questioning."

Ginny was looking at Skylar. "Is it hot in here?"

"What has that to do with anything?" her father asked. "And, no, it isn't, to answer your question."

"Are you sick, Skylar?" Ginny asked. "You look clammy."

"Eat your egg," Calder urged Skylar.

"Who else knows how to open that safe?" Tom asked.

"Besides myself, Mrs. Whitfield, Vance Calder, and Judge Ferris."

Ginny said, "And me."

"You?"

"Sure. When I was eight years old I kept my best agates in it all summer. I was damned if I'd let Louise

Uglythorpe get hold of them. One way or another."

"Is this true?" Wayne asked.

"Oh, Dad," Calder said. "I've been in and out of that safe all my livelong life. I hid pictures of Billy and Tom naked in it when we were ten years old. So the servants wouldn't see them. Those pictures I snuck of them in the pool house."

"They were posing," Ginny said.

"You've never seen them."

"I have, too. Where do you suppose they are now?"

"You'd better not have them," Tom said.

"I've borrowed some of Mother's jewelry for parties lots of times. She's never even known it."

"You have?"

Tom said to Ginny, "Actually, I'd like to see those pictures."

"What are you offering?" Ginny asked Tom.

Calder said, "There's no more mystery to that safe than there was to Who Killed Nicole Simpson."

"My, my." Wayne looked at the windows. "Your grandfather Calder installed that safe, the original unit."

"And isn't that safe one of the places Granpop Calder hid his Jameson's whiskey?" Calder said. "Probably one fifth of the thirsty masses this side of the Canadian border know how to get in and out of that safe."

"Republicans, anyway," Ginny said.

"Jon?" his father asked.

"Yes?"

"I don't hear you admitting you know how to access that safe."

Jon shrugged. "Once or twice I've closed the safe, when I've found it open."

"And once or twice have you opened the safe, when you found it closed?"

Jon smiled.

Calder asked, "Don't you like soft-boiled eggs, Skylar?"

Lacey entered the dining room and slid directly into her seat at her end of the table. "If anyone is wondering, I have a hair appointment for two o'clock. So many people coming to this party, they actually had to fit me in for my usual appointment. I had to ask! Can you imagine?" Obadiah poured her coffee. "Obadiah, aren't those caterers a little late? Perhaps you should call them."

"Yes, ma'am."

"Aunt Lacey," Skylar said, "I sure am miserable someone stole your diamond thingies."

Lacey said, "I can't imagine why anyone else would want them. I've just been telling the police how highly I regard their sentimental value, since my husband gave them to me." She beamed down the table at the Sports Results.

"For a Southerner," Calder said, "supposedly used to the heat, Skylar, you certainly sweat a lot in a cool room in the Northeast."

Lacey asked, "Is our air-conditioning inadequate to your needs, Skylar?"

"More than adequate, ma'am. We don't have air-conditioning at home."

"No," Jon said. "They don't. All they have are people flappin' their lips all sides of you about when the breeze might come up."

"By the way, Skylar," Lacey said, "the police want to interview you next."

"The police want to question me? Oh, Lord."

"Calder and Tom, you two are supposed to be at

the club playing in the golf tournament. Tee-off time was a half hour ago."

They rose from the table. "We're on our way." Calder giggled. "Too bad to waste a perfectly good soft-boiled egg."

"Everybody today please try to stay out of the way of the servants," Lacey asked. "They have enough to do with two hundred people coming tonight. Why don't you take Skylar to lunch at the club with you?"

When the ambassador's wife, followed by the ambassador, entered the room, the men rose from their seats.

Immediately, the ambassador put his hand on the back of Skylar's neck. He gestured with his right hand. "Hunker, then tap, hunker, then tap, then wreck!" He laughed.

"Yes, sir. You've got that right."

"Good morning!" the ambassador said to all others.

Skylar asked, "Where are the police?"

Jon said, "I'll go with you, Skylar."

"Wayne," the ambassador said, "there is no need for you to engage police protection for me. There is nothing revolutionary going on in my country. . . ."

"Hear that?" Jon quietly asked Skylar in the corridor outside the dining room. "There's nothing revolutionary going on in his country. That's only one thing wrong with it."

"Jon? Will you all have to pack up and sell off the place?"

"What place? Here? Why do you ask that?"

"Man, you all just lost ten fortunes, if you lost one! Jonesy told me last night those diamonds your daddy rented from the bank cost something like five million dollars."

"Rented them from a bank? What gave you the idea he rented them from a bank?"

"If he didn't rent them from the bank, how come the bank sent along a man to watch over them?"

"My father bought those particular jewels for my mother years ago. They belong to her. They're kept in the bank because the bank's safes are safer than our safe. As you see."

"I don't understand word one of all this. You all wake up one fine morning and discover you've been robbed of more money than I've ever heard of and, and . . ."

"You're spluttering, Skylar."

"And you don't even cancel a big ol' party? Wouldn't you at least postpone it until the diamonds are found?"

"Mother has other jewelry to wear."

"Calder and Tom What's-his-name go off to play a game of golf?"

"Labor Day Tournament. There's one every year."

"I mean, why aren't you all turnin' over every dust mote lookin' for those gembobs? Here your mother was just braggin' on their sentimental value. . . ."

"The cops will do all that. Don't worry. The jewelry is insured."

"Who?" Skylar asked shaking his head, amazed. "Me, worry?"

Chapter 5

"Where are the jewels?" Lieutenant John Cobb, the police detective, asked Skylar. "We've searched the bedroom you and your cousin Jonathan shared last night. And your luggage. You play the trumpet, huh? The exercise equipment that kid has got! Better than the Police Academy's. Are you and Jonathan friends? I heard he spent time with you earlier this summer, at your parents' farm in Tennessee. Sorry I asked him to wait outside while I question you. You're not afraid of me asking you some questions, are you, without your cousin present? How come you're sweating so much? It's not hot in here. I also heard you and your cousin are maybe not such very good friends, maybe even hate each other. At least you sent him home from Tennessee with a fat lip or something. What do you think of these people here? Your girl cousins, uncle, aunt? Hate them, too? One's snootier than the next. Put their noses up at my questioning them. Well, it's their damned jewels that are missing. Why are you shaking? Are those needle marks on your legs? How long have you been shooting up? So you arrived by bus yesterday afternoon from Tennessee? What will the police in your hometown tell me about you when I call them this afternoon? Ever been accused of a felony before?"

Sitting on the other side of his uncle's desk from the police lieutenant, Skylar took a deep breath. "Well, sir, I swanee down my back! You're the fastest-talkin' Yankee sombitch I've met yet! I swear!"

"What?"

Her chin on her hands on the edge of the desk surface, a police officer watched the reel of tape revolve in a recorder. She glanced at Skylar and smiled.

"Didn't your mama never teach you no manners? Where I come from, you'd have a mouthful of fist in the first five minutes of hittin' town, policeman or no, and the church ladies would take up a burial collection for you the first day you mentioned you hoped to stay a week. And I tell you no lies!"

The lieutenant straightened his back. He leaned forward and put his forearms on the desk. "What did I say that bothered you the most?"

"Calling my family snooty."

"Aren't they?"

"They're my family."

"They don't much like you, Skylar."

"That makes no mind, what we may think of each other. That's none of anybody's business outside the family."

"You don't even know these people, Skylar. You want to hear what your cousin Calder says about you?"

"They're family. And speakin' of family, I'd know you for a Cobb anywhere. There's some Cobbs in the county next to us—"

"So, are you and Jonathan friends, or not?"

"None of your business."

"Are those needle marks on your legs?"

"Don't you know tick bites when you see 'em? Man, you don't know much." Skylar scratched vigorously. "You kinda miss 'em when they're gone."

"Jon picked you up at the bus terminal yesterday afternoon?"

"He did."

"You drove straight home?"

"He did. Not that I'm sayin' any of your roads around here run straight."

"What did you do when you got home—I mean, here, to Paxton Landing?"

"Met my uncle. In the study. Chatted with him briefly."

"About what?"

Skylar hesitated. "Uncle Wayne congratulated me for winning a scholarship to Knightsbridge College of Music."

"Then what?"

"Jon brought me to Aunt Lacey's bedroom. Met her. And Cousin Calder, Cousin Ginny, and Jonesy, who I guess is Jon's girlfriend. Goes to Harvard with him or something."

"Did you chat with them?"

"Not much. They were playin' with these gembobs that were on the bedspread."

"The jewels that are missing?"

"I guess."

"Can you describe them to me?"

"A hat thing—"

"A tiara."

"A big necklace, a wide bracelet, and earbobs."

"'Earbobs.' Can you tell me what kind of gems they were?"

"Diamonds, mostly."

"What else? Emeralds, rubies . . . ?"

"Lieutenant Cobb, I don't know a ruby from a pinto bean."

"You ever seen jewelry like that before, Skylar?"

"No, sir. I sure haven't. My mama has a pearl necklace my daddy gave her on their fifteenth wedding anniversary. Two strands. She wears it everywhere."

"What did you think of the jewelry you saw on your aunt Lacey's bed last night?"

"Not much. They're ladies' things. Doubt you could catch much crappie with them."

"'Crappie'? What's crappie?"

"A fish."

"Sounds good. Guess I won't ask you what you use for sauce on a crappie. How much did you think the jewelry you saw might be worth?"

"I worried they might be worth a lot, the way the women were oooin' and aaain' over 'em."

"Like how much?"

"Two, three thousand dollars."

"Are you serious?"

"Yes, sir."

"What do you mean you 'worried' how much they might be worth?"

"Where I come from, for two, three thousand dollars you could buy five, six healthy calves. That's what any sensible person would buy if he had that kind of money to spare."

"Did you hear anything about where the jewelry was to be kept?"

"No, sir. I don't know anything about safes. I still don't know where the safe is." Skylar could see nothing behind the desk that could have been a safe. There was nothing at all in front of or on the walnut-paneled wall. Along the baseboard there was a small red light.

"I'm not used to livin' in a bank. My folks keep their important papers in a fireproof box under their bed, good to eighteen hundred degrees Fahrenheit."

"Now do you know how much that jewelry is worth?"

"Last night, Jonesy mentioned those jewels might be worth as much as five million dollars. Although I can scarcely credit it."

"That'd buy a lot of calves, right? So, in fact, by the time the jewelry was stolen last night, you did know how much it was worth. After seeing the jewelry, what did you do?"

"Dumped my suitcase in Jon's room. We horsed around in the swimming pool for a while. Then he doodled me up in his clothes for dinner. After dinner I talked with Jonesy on the terrace a few minutes, called my parents from Jon's room, went to bed, oh, about ten-fifteen."

Lieutenant Cobb wrote on his pad of paper, "Search the poolhouse, & around the pool."

"Besides the pool area, have you been anywhere else around the estate?"

"No, sir."

"Did you leave your bed during the night?"

"Slept like a rattler on a warm rock."

"Skylar, since meeting your uncle yesterday afternoon, at any point since have you returned to this room?"

"No, sir."

"And you've never been in this house before?"

"Never been in New England before. Wasn't too keen to come this time."

"Okay, Skylar." Hands folded on the top of his head, Lieutenant Cobb sat back in the desk chair. "You're in over your head, aren't you?"

"What say you?"

"At first you thought the jewelry was worth only a few thousand dollars. I would say you listened pretty closely as to where it was to be stored. Then, when you were told how much the jewelry was worth—"

"Lieutenant Cobb, this is exactly why I'm sweatin' this. A poor relation from the South shows up only a few hours before jewelry goes missin' and it's as natural as fartin' after beans you think he's the thief. I'm not foolin' myself. I am a relative, but bein' a Southerner, I know I'm more of a foreigner here than even that ambassador from Whereverland. You Yankees have been blamin' Southerners for the woes of the world goin' on three hundred years now."

"Are you going to refight the Civil War with me?"

"You mean the Brothers' War?"

"You're a farm boy whose only talent seems to be blowin' air through a pipe with valves on it. You have to resent these people, their wealth, education, sophistication, servants. . . . Maybe you think a little of what is theirs ought to be yours?"

"I knew my uncle was rich," Skylar said. "I didn't know he was rich enough to spend five million good American dollars on a bridle for his wife. I didn't know anyone was that rich. But I don't care about that. In Greendowns County, my family is considered among the nicest folks around. You don't know that, is what worries me. We have land, and both my mama and daddy work. I'm proud of them. And I'm proud to tell you I know a whole lot of things most of these people here don't know."

"Like what?"

"Well . . ."

"How to drug a security guard and open a locked safe? I've checked some of the bathrooms in this house, as you probably have, too. There are plenty of sedatives in the medicine chests."

"I know a tick bite when I see one."

"Okay, Skylar. If you tell me where the jewelry is today and give it back, I promise this whole matter will be forgotten, at least by the law. Who knows? Your uncle might even be so relieved he'd slip you a present of two or three thousand dollars. A reward for your help, we'll call it."

Skylar stood up. "All I got to say to you, Lieutenant Cobb, is: Don't leave town. And if you do, I strongly suggest you stay out of Tennessee."

"Send your cousin in."

Far more relaxed than his cousin, Jon sat in the chair Skylar had vacated.

"Use drugs?" Lieutenant Cobb asked.

"No."

"Gamble?"

"No."

"Got a girl in trouble?"

"No."

"Doing well at college?"

"Yes."

"In debt?"

"No."

"Need money for any purpose?"

"I've got money."

"Not five million of your own."

"How would you know?"

"Have you?"

"None of your business."

"Snooty, snooty. Let's just do a rundown of some of the people here last night. The butler?"

"Obadiah. He's from northern India, originally. He's been with us four or five years. Before that, he was with my uncle."

"Vance Calder?"

"Yes."

"Why did he leave your uncle and come to work for you folks?"

"He said he wanted more of a family environment."

"And your uncle Vance is an aging playboy, right?"

Jon said nothing.

"The cook, Mrs. Watts?"

"She's been with us since before I was born."

"You know anything about her personal life?"

"I doubt she has one."

"And there are three maids."

Jon covered his mouth when he yawned. "Such come and go. Always have. Always will. As far as I know they're all named Mary."

"Jonathan, we're assuming this robbery is an inside job. Whoever took the jewelry knew it was here, that it was in the safe, how to get into the safe."

"A child can get in and out of that safe. It's been tarted up with an electronic alarm system, but the basic unit is very old."

"Can you get into and out of that safe?"

"Sure."

"None of the servants has a police record of any kind. Needless to say, neither has the security guard."

"There's always a first time for anything."

"I don't see Judge Ferris, a seventy-year-old widower, pinching the gems. I would not be quick to accuse an ambassador or his wife of such a crime."

"Why not?"

"What did you do after dinner last night?"

"Tom and I played billiards. We each had a cognac. We played until about eleven. Then I went into the living room and said good night to people, and went upstairs to bed."

"Was your cousin already in bed?"

"Yes."

"This young woman, Jones—"

"Joan Appleyard. She's called Jonesy."

"Didn't you spend any time with her after dinner?"

"No."

"Isn't she your girlfriend?"

"Yes. She was in the living room playing bridge with my mother and the ambassador and his wife."

"Did you kiss Jonesy good night?"

"Why do you ask that?"

"Did you go to her room during the night?"

"No. What has this to do with anything?"

"Might you marry this Jonesy?"

"Might. We're not engaged."

"Considering your ages, it doesn't seem a very passionate affair."

"Jonesy and I have known each other for years. We spent time together yesterday afternoon."

"At any point during the night did you leave your bed?"

"No. Maybe to use the bathroom. I don't remember."

"Do you know if Skylar left your room?"

"No. Lieutenant Cobb, I don't usually drink. I had several glasses of wine at dinner, one or two brandies with Tom. Once I went to sleep, nothing woke me up."

"This Tom you're talking about. Tom Palmer? Is he

Calder's boyfriend? I mean, her main squeeze?"

"I guess. He's also someone we've known all our lives."

"He stayed by himself in a small guest room. Never left his room. Jonesy stayed in a small bedroom. You never left your room. For healthy young people, I must say you all seem remarkably abstinent. And your parents have separate bedrooms."

"There's nothing you can do between twelve and six you can't do between six and twelve."

"Which brings us to Skylar. What do you think of him?"

"I got to know him a little bit when I was in Tennessee this summer."

"Which doesn't answer the question as to what you think of him."

"Not much, at first. Then I discovered he's a phony."

"Beg pardon?"

"He puts on the Southern humility and good old boy stuff, but he's about as dumb as a fox."

"You mean he's very clever?"

"Yes. Very resourceful. He fools you."

"Clever enough to steal the jewelry?"

"Sure."

"You believe he did?"

"No."

"Why not? He arrives at five o'clock in the afternoon, sees the jewelry, later discovers how much it's worth; within twelve hours the jewelry is missing."

"Why would he want it?"

"Why would he want five million dollars?"

"He wouldn't know what to do with the jewelry, how to turn it into cash."

"Frequently that doesn't stop people from taking things."

"Listen, Lieutenant, Skylar comes from a world where people don't lock their houses, their cars—"

"There are no robberies in Tennessee?"

"I suppose there are. But he wouldn't be able to dispose of the jewelry."

"Not right away, maybe. Perhaps he plans to keep it a few years. That would be clever."

"I don't see Skylar as a thief."

"There are thieves who have not been known to steal before. As you said, there's a first time for everything. In this case, resentment might be as much a motive as greed."

"Resentment?"

"Sure. This farm boy comes to visit his rich cousins, sees how very much you all have, this glorious estate on the river, swimming pool, fancy cars, servants. I would say Calder, maybe your mother, maybe all of you look down your noses at the way he talks, and dresses, and looks. Surely Calder puts him down, snubs him. As you said, he's not stupid. You think he doesn't realize this?"

"So he'd steal the jewelry because we laugh at him a little bit?" Jon looked aside. "Maybe. He's more sensitive than he seems."

"If he stole the jewelry, where would he have hidden it?"

"How would I know?"

"Keep your eyes open, will you?"

"Of course."

"Where did Ms. Appleyard go so early this morning?"

"I don't know."

"She mentioned nothing to you about going somewhere at dawn?"

"No, she didn't."

"Wouldn't she be concerned you might worry about her taking off that way?"

"I'm not worried about her."

"What you mean," Lieutenant Cobb said, smiling at the self-assured young man, "is you're not concerned about her. Nor she you."

Chapter 6

"I appreciate your making time for me on a Saturday morning," Jonesy said. "I had this dream last night I want to tell you about. Very disturbing."

Although there was a desk in her homey Cambridge office, Dr. MacBride did not sit behind it. Legs crossed beneath her long linen skirt, notebook in her lap, she sat in a flowery wing-backed chair, as did Jonesy.

"Why disturbing?" she asked.

Dr. MacBride had already started the tape recorder on her desk.

"It was so real," Jonesy said. "I never remember having a dream so real."

"Tell me."

"Last night I was in the bed in the guest room I usually use out at Paxton Landing."

"Is this the dream? Or did you stay at Paxton Landing last night?"

"I stayed at Paxton Landing last night. It's just a

little bedroom. It used to be a sewing room. Yes, this is the dream."

"You dreamed you were asleep in the bed in that room while you were asleep in the bed in that room? Have I got that right?"

"Yes."

"About what time was this? Any idea?"

"Just before dawn."

"Okay. And you had been asleep."

"I was asleep. I heard the door to the corridor open. I looked toward the door. I saw a slim, totally naked body, a young man, standing there in the open door. He was backlit by the dim lights in the corridor. Broad shoulders, slim hips, long, muscular, slim arms and legs. I saw his nose and jaw in profile. His head was turned, maybe listening. His left hand was on the outside doorknob. His body turned as he closed the door quietly.

"In profile, the light picked up the tanned skin of his chest and flat stomach and thighs."

"What light?"

"There was a dim, doll-shaped lamp on the dressing table by the door I had left on."

"I take it this young man wasn't Jon."

"No. It was Jon's cousin. Skylar."

"What did you do? Why didn't you scream?"

"I was too surprised. I was fascinated. He was so beautiful."

"He was entirely naked? He had come through the house to your room entirely naked?"

"Must have. I didn't tell you something. When he turned I saw his penis in profile. It shone, somehow, as if it were wet or something. Long, it stuck straight out from his body.

"Slowly his head turned. He faced me in the bed.

"Walking on the balls of his feet, taking slow, giant strides, he came across the room to me.

"With his left hand, slowly he stripped the blanket and sheet off my body.

"And looked at me. I mean, looked at me. Totally. All of me. His face was beautiful, half-smiling. Charmed, you know?"

Doctor MacBride sat straighter in her chair. She re-crossed her legs. "Were you naked in bed?"

"Of course. I never wear nightclothes, unless it's freezing. A warm summer's night . . ."

"Who is Skylar? I didn't know Jon had a cousin."

"Skylar Whitfield. He arrived from Tennessee yesterday afternoon. He's matriculating at Knightsbridge School of Music next week. He plays the trumpet. He's never been here before."

"So yesterday afternoon was the first you ever saw of him?"

"Yes."

"Were you attracted to him?"

"Oh, yes. Very. Physically, very. Something in the way he stands, moves, looks at you. He exudes sex."

"What does that mean, to you? 'Exudes sex' . . ."

"His body, his eyes, shoot out waves of electricity. I don't know. He's so aware he's a male. And he seems so damned happy about it, I mean about being a male. I guess I haven't seen much of that in my life. You know, there's nothing the least ashamed about him. And there's something in him that also says, 'You're a female. Isn't that nice!' " Jonesy giggled.

"Did he come on to you last night, I mean, during the evening?"

"No. Not really. I think that's just the way he is. He asked me if I was Jon's girlfriend."

"And you said yes?"

"I said something. I don't remember what."

"Go on."

"I started to try to roll off the bed, to my right, to get away from him.

"Quickly he put the palms of his hands on my shoulders. He pinned my shoulders to the bed.

"Kneeling, one leg either side of me, he sort of sat on my hips. The creases across his stomach were no deeper than a hair."

"You could see all that from that little light?"

"I could see. Dawn light was beginning to come through the window. His penis reached a good way up my stomach."

"Why didn't you scream?"

"Because his mouth was on mine. Lightly at first. His lips slid around mine. I was breathing hard already. He smelled so good. Like I've never smelled from a man before. Nothing like cologne."

"Of what did he smell?"

"Skin. Sunlight on skin. Clean sweat. Outdoors. He smelled of outdoors. Of woods, you know, the fresh air you sometimes taste in the woods. He smelled so real.

"Without hurting at all, his mouth opened mine. Still he slid his lips around on mine. Then his tongue came into my mouth. His tongue lifted my tongue, and then went around and around my tongue, under, over, along the sides."

"Didn't you resist? Do anything?"

"I was resisting. I was wriggling around, raising one of my hips, then the other, trying to get him off me. I was pounding his back muscles with my fists. It was like hitting smooth wood. Except all the muscles under his tight skin were moving somehow. I reached my arms, my hands, down and tried to tear his ass cheeks apart."

"Didn't he stop?"

"No. It was wonderful. Then his hipbone was rubbing up and down in my crotch. I think I came right then."

"He must be slim."

"Then his mouth left mine. His tongue began to play with my left nipple, so gently at first."

"Your mouth was free. Why didn't you cry out?"

"I was choking, of something, somehow. My throat was so tight."

"Did he have a hand on your throat?"

"No. His left hand was gently playing with my right breast."

"Were you crying?"

"I think I was. My face was wet, cool with tears. I was sweating. We both were. His muscles were sliding over me. Then one of his fingers, then, after a while, two of his fingers, then three of his fingers entered me. Could I have come three times?"

"I don't know. Could you?"

"How could I have all these orgasms in a dream, when I haven't in fact?"

"A dream?"

"Pressing the back of my head onto my pillow, my back was arched like never before. I wanted him to enter me so much."

"And did he? Just how did he do that?"

"He didn't. I did. I think. His fingers still in me, I discovered he was kneeling, his knees right against my crotch. Then his hands picked up my hips. He slid my hips up his thighs. Then he put his forearms behind my back, his fingers on my shoulders. He lifted me up. All of a sudden there was fresh air. I was gulping. I rubbed my face against his neck, his throat.

"I was sort of in his lap, sitting on his thighs. I don't know.

"I put the tip of his penis in me.

"He couldn't move much. But I came again.

"In this wonderful motion, somehow he separated his knees, my thighs, and slowly came down on me. Into me, you know what I mean? Deep, deep into me. He stretched his legs full-length along mine.

"At first he used a rotating motion, you know what I mean? Rotating his hips? Then, only after I clasped my ankles together behind his back did he begin to thrust and thrust and thrust."

Dr. MacBride said, "I'm expected in Wellfleet for lunch."

"After, we lay together a while, breathing hard, cooling off. One of his legs was across my stomach. His forearm was across my breasts.

"After a while, he got up, kissed me on the cheek, and quietly, on the balls of his feet, strode out of the room just as he had entered.

"He had never said a word, through all that.

"I don't know if I fell asleep for a few moments, or passed out. Or if that was when I woke up."

"But you said you were asleep?"

"Yes. The bed was totally messed up. And I'm a neat sleeper. The sheet was soaking wet.

"I'd never felt so exhausted in my life. I was tired in every muscle.

"Anyway, I couldn't sleep anymore. I got off the bed, staggered to the shower, and got dressed. I came straight into town. Waiting to call you at nine o'clock, would you believe I ate six doughnuts? I've never eaten six doughnuts at one time before in my life."

"Joan, are you sure you dreamed all this?"

"What else?"

"I don't know. Usually such dreams are not in such detail. You are even able to describe to me his unusual smell. Dreams don't last that long. The dawn rising through your window. It all seems so real."

"Surreal?"

"No. So real. I said 'So real.' "

"I know. That's why I came to see you."

"Why? Why did you come to see me? This can't be the first erotic dream you've ever had. If that's what happened."

"How come I can have multiple orgasms in bed by myself when I don't when I'm really making love?"

"Joan, I'm not at all sure you were in bed by yourself. Can you describe specific things about this boy's body?"

Jonesy smiled. "I already have, haven't I?"

"Specific things. Birthmarks. Wounds."

"He has some tick bites on his lower legs. One below his belly button."

"Have you ever seen this boy naked before?"

"No. I just met him last night."

"Joan, I think I'd better send you over to the clinic. Rape tests. Make sure all this was a dream."

"You can't. I mean, I can't."

"Why not?"

"I did make love yesterday afternoon."

"With Jon?"

"They're cousins."

"That wouldn't matter. DNA tests on semen are very precise. Are you taking your contraceptive pills?"

"Yes."

"What about protecting yourself otherwise?"

"Jon and I . . . neither of us is seeing anyone else . . . sexually."

"Still . . ."

"I trust Jon."

"I would like to establish whether you were raped last night. This morning. Do you really believe that was all a dream?"

"I don't know. I can't believe I messed the bed up so much myself. I never have before. Or wore myself out so much. How is it possible? You're right. It all seemed so real."

"I think if you were convinced it was all a dream you wouldn't have rushed intown on Labor Day weekend Saturday morning to see me. Now, would you?"

"I don't know."

"Joan, what do you think we ought do about this? You won't let me send you to the clinic for tests?"

"No."

Dr. MacBride said, "Then I just don't know."

Jonesy said, "I don't either."

Chapter 7

"It's usually better to paddle upstream first," Ginny advised him. "Especially when a picnic is involved."

In her bikini and sneakers, she sat in the front of the canoe facing backward. A knapsack was at her feet.

"Okay." Pushing off from the riverbank, Skylar stepped into the canoe. "Although I think I knew that."

"I'll show you the folly. My favorite place. It's a mile or two upstream. Then we can go out to my most favorite place, this tiny island, where we can have the picnic."

Paddling away from the rocky, log-strewn riverbank, Skylar looked back across his right shoulder at a strange edifice built half on land and half over the river. The walls of the first floor seemed entirely of glass. The windows of the second floor were small and round. The roof over the second floor had an oddly nautical look.

"That's our boathouse," Ginny said. "Dad had it

rebuilt a few years ago. Now it's rented out."

"You all need the rent?"

"It was either that or tear it down. I don't know. Maybe he thought someday it would be a starter house for us as we got married, Jon and Jonesy, or Calder and Tom."

"Or Ginny and—?"

"I'd say you, if you weren't my cousin."

"You in love with me?"

"I'll say." Through sunlight she squinted at Skylar in shorts and sneakers paddling the canoe. "You're a mighty healthy-lookin' beast, Skylar."

"I am a beast. I bay at the moon, when it's full. Aa-oouuu!"

"That's all right. A woman should be able to put up with almost anything from a man, if it happens only once a month. A man has to, from a woman. Right?"

"Most months."

"Blue moon," Ginny sang.

"How do you know that song?"

"Dad plays old records once in a while."

"He does?"

"Does that surprise you?"

Skylar turned the canoe upstream. "I don't see Uncle Wayne doing anything . . . I don't know . . . like that—listening to music."

"You think he's a cold fish? Most do."

"I didn't say that."

"Come to supper some Thursday night. The servants have the day off, until midnight. So Thursdays traditionally are sort of a family night. Without servants and other people around, Dad sometimes almost relaxes. Even more so since he had that heart surgery."

"Your dad had heart surgery? When?"

"Soon after Jon got home. Late June, July. He's been out of pocket most of the summer."

"No one ever told us that."

"Why should we?"

"Family."

"Sure. So your folks would have sent my dad a pot of flowers and my mother would have written your folks a thank-you note. . . . All that only benefits florists, wire services, and the post office."

"Try not to be so sentimental, Ginny."

"Anyway, on your typical Thursday nights, everything else being all right, sometimes Dad talks to us as if we are something other than first lieutenants. Sometimes he even listens to us. Sometimes you can hear a little Southern in his accent. Sometimes he plays music. Fact is, sometimes I've even seen him dance my mother around the room. Although not lately."

"And you know what a blue moon is."

"You think all Yankees are stupid?"

"Trying not to think about it."

"Your girlfriend was murdered this summer."

"That I really try not to think about."

"Sorry. Didn't Jon mention to us another girl, the one you really grew up with—"

"Please?"

"Okay. So . . ." Ginny trailed her fingers in the water. "Despite my wild and passionate love for you, I guess my first husband will have to be Alex Broadbent."

"Who's Alex Broadbent? Some sexy thirty-two-year-old movie actor who plays a teenager?"

Ginny giggled. "No. He lives in the boathouse, with his wife. With lots of other people comin' and goin', day and night. Real interesting people. Artists. Experimental musicians, writers, painters, photographers. A few politicians. My mother calls them 'Alex's flotilla.' He's a critic for the Boston newspaper."

"But what is he a critic of?"

"Music, books, movies, art. Politics."

"He knows enough about all that?"

"No one ever says he doesn't. Point is, he does things with his columns. He solves problems. He listens to everybody, reports just what they say, then makes a suggestion, or asks the obvious question, or something."

"And people respond to that?"

"You bet they do. With money for good causes. With legislation."

"Why? Why should they believe him?"

" 'Cause what he writes makes sense. He can be terribly witty, but he's never just foolin' around, if you know what I mean. And because everybody knows he has never once used the money or power for his own purposes. Or to be mean. That's what Dad says."

"Your father respects him?"

"That's why Alex is living in our boathouse. I guess he doesn't make much money off his column."

Skylar smiled. *So Alex Broadbent has been bought by one person—my uncle, Wayne Whitfield.* "How old is he?"

"Early thirties."

"Didn't I just hear you say Mr. Broadbent has a wife? How can you plan to marry him?"

"Mother says everybody thought Diane brilliant at first, because she said nothing. They thought she was thinking. Then she took some college courses. And began talking. That was the end of her." Ginny's eyes ran over the tops of the trees along the riverbank. "That marriage can't last long. The more she talks, the dumber she seems."

"And your talk is brilliant?"

"It isn't?"

"Whose place is that over there?" They were passing, on their left bank, a large white-painted brick house on a few acres of lawn.

"The Uglythorpes."

"That's not their real name."

"Certainly it is. Louise Uglythorpe goes to school with me. We're dear friends. Hate her guts."

"Why?"

" 'Cause I can't talk her out of beating me at most everything. No matter how hard I try. From spelling to jumping horses, she sneaks around behind my back and works just that little bit harder than I do."

Skylar laughed. "At least you're honest about it."

Ginny laughed, too. "At the club's junior tennis tournament last week, I spiked her lemonade with vodka. I thought the jerk would at least know what vodka tastes like. She *is* thirteen years old. Man, I didn't expect her to drink it all down."

"What happened?"

"She won."

Looking behind her, Ginny guided Skylar out of the sunlight of the river into the shade of the bank. "Run the bow up there, Skylar, see? Where there are no rocks. Run her nose a little up the bank. It's soft. That way we won't get our feet wet."

"Yes, ma'am."

Above them on the bank, by itself, stood a tower of gray stone.

As they walked up to it, Ginny said, "This was built by Judge Ferris's grandfather, who was also Judge Ferris. That family's been sitting so long, if it weren't for golf, they couldn't walk." She looked up at Skylar's face. "You like that joke?"

He laughed. "Sure."

"My uncle Vance made up that joke. He uses it quite a lot."

At the tower's base an iron door was ajar. Its top hinge was broken.

Inside, the stone floor sparkled with shards of broken glass. Seven or eight beer cans were piled against the wall. There was what was left of a cot mattress. A few of the condoms on the floor (two blue, one red) looked recent.

Skylar asked, "This where you bring all your friends?"

Ginny leading, they climbed the stone steps spiraling around the wall of the tower. "Old Judge Ferris built this late last century. I guess he thought the ladies would carry their tea parties up here on hot summer days to catch the breeze. Or their butlers would. I believe a lot of china broke against that floor down there."

The top of the tower was three meters in diameter. The wall around it was only one meter high.

"The first real battle of The War took place down there." Ginny pointed south.

"What war?"

"The American Revolution."

"Where I come from when we say 'The War' we mean The War Between the States."

"Anything here remind you of Tennessee, Skylar? Even a little bit?"

He looked on all sides of him, at houses and lawns

visible among the green trees, the blue river unevenly separating the landscape, the hills to the west. "There's more yellow in our green," he said.

"Are you homesick, Skylar?"

"More than I thought."

"Why do you suppose that is?"

"I don't want to generalize."

"Go ahead. No one's listening."

"That's one of the points. No one's listening." Skylar said, "I guess a difference in people is in what we say no to. Instead of listening, you all seem to be just waiting to break in and say no to whatever anyone else is saying."

"You find us intolerant? Rejecting? I guess you've got reason to."

"I haven't been here a full day yet, and I've been accused of stealing five million dollars or something from my family."

"Actually accused?"

"Yeah. That policeman barefaced accused me. Do your family really think I stole those jewels?"

"Mostly."

"And the servants?"

"Yes."

"Somehow what I am got turned into a dinner joke among a passel of strangers. I guess I shouldn't have tried to entertain the people on that long bus ride. I got that ambassador feller at dinner last night educatin' me on something that interested him, and me, and Jonesy said I was bein' rude somehow. I could tell I annoyed your mother."

"And what do you folks say no to?"

"Not listening. Meanness. Hate to tell you this, Cousin Ginny, but most of the folks I know in the South don't want their kids to come north to school.

They're afraid we'll learn Northern manners."

"Is that true?"

"Yes."

"I liked your friend Dufus."

"No, you didn't."

"Well, I didn't understand much of what he said."

"He spent a day here and came wingin' home. Doubt you'll ever see Dufus again much north of the tobacco barns."

"It must have been real hard for my daddy to adjust, when he came north. I'm just realizing that."

"He must have wanted some things real bad."

"Strange that college you're going to, Knightsbridge, requires you to register on Labor Day."

"I guess they want us musicians to get used to workin' on holidays."

"Do you want that real bad, Skylar? I mean, to be a professional musician?"

"At this moment, I don't know."

"Well, I like you, Skylar. Maybe you ought to go home, back south. Before we turn your manners bad."

"Maybe I will," Skylar said. "Now I've got the family jewelry, why not?"

"Come on." Ginny took his hand. "I want to show you our secret."

At the base of the tower was a stone bulkhead. Seeing it, one most likely would assume it was a small cistern.

Ginny tugged its iron cover along the grooves in the top until the opening was half exposed.

Then she walked to the bulkhead's other side. "Come on."

"Well, I'll be . . ." Skylar followed Ginny down narrow stone steps. "A tower with a basement. Sure you're not leading me into a dungeon? Honest, Ginny, I didn't take your mama's gembobs!"

"I know."

By the time he reached the bottom of the steps Ginny had lit a hurricane lantern.

"Why," Skylar said, "this place has got everythin' 'cept whips and chains!"

The circular walls were wet stone. The area was very cool and smelled strongly of damp earth.

"I'll be damned," Skylar said. "This place really is a dungeon. You Yankees think of everything. How many of my Confederate cousins you expect are buried under this floor?"

The uneven stone floor was swept clean. There was even a dull old round rag rug in the middle.

"Story is"—Ginny lifted the lamp onto a peg jammed between two wall stones—"that this is the real reason old Judge Ferris built this folly. He stored guns and ammunition here in case there was a populist uprising or something."

"You Yankees are the most scarified people. . . ."

"I think it more likely he stored wine here. But twice the place was prepared as a bomb shelter, once during World War Two and again, later, during the Cold War."

Around some of the circumference of the walls were the remnants of shelves. There were a few cartons of food and soft drinks even now on the shelves. There were rusting two-hundred-gallon kegs, with spigots.

And there were two tiers of bunk beds. Neatly folded were two bedrolls.

Ginny sat on one of the two chairs at the small, round table in the center.

"How come this place is so clean?" Skylar asked. "Who uses it?"

"Oh, sometimes Louise Uglythorpe and I do."

She patted the table. "We sit here and play cards and talk, have cupcake orgies. You know . . ." She grinned. "When we feel like crawlin' back into the womb."

Skylar watched the light from the hurricane lantern flickering on the whites of his cousin's eyes. "I thought you hated Louise Uglythorpe."

"I do." Her fingers and arms taut, Ginny made the motion of choking someone. "I'd like to throttle the little bitch. I probably will someday. Real soon."

"Then how come—?"

"We all have our problems," Ginny said. "Isn't that right? Louise has a new stepdaddy. Mr. Nance. Mr. Edward Nance. You ever hear of him?"

"No. Why should I?"

"He was a star basketball coach or something."

"Louise isn't taking his name?"

"He's not adopting her."

"Why not?"

"She's an Uglythorpe heiress. Anyway, he's always talking about how she's his responsibility now, and he must teach her things, educate her. You know?" Now Ginny was running her thumbs along her fingertips. "Sometimes he tries to follow us through the woods, to see where we're going? We've managed to lose him every time, even in daylight, so far."

"Who *does* know about this place?" Skylar asked.

"Know about it?" Ginny stuck the tip of her thumb into her mouth. "Lots of people know about it. Everybody's forgotten about it, though. You mean, who knows Louise and I are using this place? No one."

"Then why are you showing me?"

"So you won't feel so rejected. So you believe I like you." Ginny stuck her thumb well into her mouth and talked through her fist. "So you'll remember you, too, can crawl back into the womb!"

"Are you glad I rescued you?" Ginny asked.

"Yes," Skylar answered. "From what?"

On an island not much bigger than a barge, mostly covered with rough rock and trees with twisted roots, they sat on a patch of hard-packed earth in the shade. Ginny was taking the picnic out of the knapsack.

After being interviewed by the police, not knowing what else to do, Skylar had returned to Jon's room. He was surprised to see the room already cleaned and made up.

After looking at Jon's books and tennis trophies, Skylar stripped to his underpants and proceeded to use Jon's exercise equipment.

Except for a few cars in the driveway he could hear through the window, the house was quiet.

Jon never returned to his room.

After forty-five minutes, Skylar was getting tired of exercising in the sepulchral silence. He was wondering what he might do next. Could do next. Should do next.

When he was bench-pressing weights in his last set of fives, Ginny entered the bedroom without knocking.

"Come on," she said. "I've asked Mrs. Watts to put together a picnic for us. You're all sweaty. You know how to paddle a canoe?"

He put the weight bar in its cradle and sat up. "Not if you do."

"I just forgot," Ginny said. "So you paddle."

On the little island, Ginny handed Skylar a bottle of root beer. "Mrs. Watts did us proud."

"What's this red stuff in the chicken salad?"

"Pimiento? Red pepper?"

Chewing, Skylar said, "Red pepper. It's good."

Ginny took an eggcup from the knapsack and placed it on the ground in front of her.

"Skylar, didn't you happen to notice they all—Calder, Tom, Jonathan—went off to the country club and left you home?"

"Is that where they went?" Skylar watched Ginny remove from the knapsack two eggs, a small silver spoon, and a small crystal salt cellar and pepper shaker. "I don't play golf."

"That's not all you do at a country club, Skylar."

"What else do you do?"

"Meet people." With the small silver spoon, Ginny was tapping around the top of the egg in the cup.

Skylar said, "Oh. I know quite a lot of people already."

Ginny lifted the top off the egg and dropped it on the ground. "Aren't you insulted?"

"I wasn't very nice to Jon Than when he first appeared in Greendowns County. I was shy of meetin' him, shy of havin' him meet my friends."

"Why?"

"I thought he might be a snob."

"Was he?"

"Yes."

"He can't think you're a snob." She salted and peppered the top of the egg.

"Maybe he thinks I'm a reverse snob. That I wouldn't like his friends."

"More likely, that his friends wouldn't like you."

"Guess playin' trumpet don't make much hay

'round here, where everyone's an ambassador, or judge, or investment banker, or butler, or whatever." He watched Ginny neatly eat her cold soft-boiled egg. "How did Uncle Wayne get so rich, anyway?"

"He didn't." She put her second egg in the eggcup. With her little spoon, she proceeded to tap around its top. "Well, he did make money, of course. Have you been to Jonathan's rooms at Harvard yet?"

"No."

"He lives in a place called Calder House. You've met my mother's brother, Vance Calder. My sister's name is my mother's family name. Some ancestor of mine gave Harvard the money to build Calder House."

"My daddy gave the Baptist church five acres to extend the cemetery."

"Your uncle Wayne, my daddy, worked for Calder Partners. Except there never had been any partners who weren't Calders."

"What were they all partners at?"

"Making money."

"Oh."

"However they could."

Skylar said, "Just makin' money? Not makin' anything real? Weird!"

"For a while there, my uncle Vance was the last male Calder. So grandfather Calder made your uncle Wayne a partner, and he married my mother, and here I am. Daddy's made a lot of money, of course, for the partnership. For himself, too, I guess." Ginny finished eating the second egg. "I guess to prove it, a few years ago he gave that mess of jewels you stole to my mother. At the same time, he made some kind of independent settlement on each of us kids."

"Okay, okay. I'll give the jewels back. If they mean that much to you all."

Ginny placed the not-very-dirty eggcup and spoon in Skylar's plastic sandwich bag and put them back in her knapsack. "Umm! That was good! Did you enjoy your picnic?"

"I'd rather have had a couple of soft-boiled eggs," he said.

And gave Ginny a wide, loving grin.

Chapter 8

Without removing her sleep mask, Lacey brought her buzzing bedside telephone receiver to her ear. In order not to disturb her newly done hair, the back of her head rested flat on the pillow.

"Obadiah." She spoke sharply. "I asked not to be disturbed. I have to have my rest before people begin arriving for the party. Has something come up you can't handle?"

"Yes, Mrs. Whitfield. There is someone on the telephone who insists she must speak to you immediately." Obadiah's English accent was northern Indian. He spoke with breathless rapidity. "A Dr. MacBride. She says she is Ms. Appleyard's psychiatrist."

Lacey hesitated. "Do you know where Ms. Appleyard is at the moment?"

"No, Mrs. Whitfield."

"All right." Lacey sighed. "Put her through."

A click. "Hello? Mrs. Whitfield?"

"Yes."

"This is Susan MacBride. I am Joan Appleyard's

psychiatrist. Joan is staying with you at Paxton Landing?"

"She was here last night. I understand she left quite early this morning. Her present whereabouts are unknown to me."

"Yes. Early this morning she came to see me in Cambridge. She told me something puzzling. Disturbing. She seemed confused. Since seeing her I have driven down to Wellfleet and lunched with friends. I haven't been able to help thinking about what she told me."

Yes, my girl, Lacey said to herself, eyes closed behind her sleep mask. And from the way you're slightly slurring your words, I'd say you had a fairly wet lunch.

"Are you there?"

"Yes."

"You also have a young man staying with you named Skylar?"

"Yes."

"Is he your nephew?"

"Yes. On my husband's side."

"Mrs. Whitfield, I'm not sure I know how to say this to you. But I thought I'd be remiss if I failed to report it to you."

Oh, get on with it, Lacey said to herself.

"A possible rape took place at your home this morning."

" 'Rape,' you say."

"I meant to say, possibly a rape took place in your home this morning."

"Will you get to the point, please?"

"Joan described to me an event in which your nephew entered her bedroom nude shortly before dawn, attacked her on her bed, and had his way with her, as people used to say, despite her protestations and struggling to get away from him."

"I should say that's rape, yes."

"However, Joan told me of this event as if it were a dream."

"A dream, indeed?"

"But her description was so vivid. She seems not sure as to whether she dreamed this event."

"If she just dreamed it, I should call it a nonevent, wouldn't you?"

"It may be her way of distancing herself emotionally from this event."

"Or it may have been a dream. Girls have such dreams."

"What disturbs me is that she told me of this dream with such great specificity. She was able to describe your nephew's body in the greatest detail, even down to where his tick bites are."

"I believe they were swimming together yesterday evening."

"They were? She described his unusual smell. Most disturbing to me, upon reflection, is that she said that while the act was ongoing, the sun rose and her room filled with light, indicating this event took place over a goodly period of time."

"Do we know how long a dream actually lasts?"

"We believe a dream happens instantaneously, within a second."

"I've never believed that."

"You're not a psychiatrist."

"How you professionals love to say that. Anything can happen in a dream, I believe, including the passage of time. Dare I assert that?"

"Mrs. Whitfield, why are you resenting me? You

seem hostile. Do you think I should not be telling you this?"

"Telling me what?"

"That your nephew may have raped my patient."

"You're a doctor. Are you able to report to me any physical evidence that a rape took place?"

"She stated that after awakening—or awakening again; she may have passed out—after the event, her bedclothes were wet from sweat and in great disarray. And she reported she was physically deeply exhausted. She refused my suggestion that she go to the clinic for an examination."

"Why? Why did she refuse?"

"Because I gather that only hours before, your son, Jonathan, had made love to her."

"Does that make sense to you? Her refusing to be examined? It doesn't to me."

"It might."

"Dr. MacBride, I'm still not sure what it is you are telling me."

"Forewarned is forearmed. I understand you do not know this nephew at all. He is newly arrived from the South. Why did he come here?"

"I suspect you're telling me Jonesy had what is vulgarly referred to among our male population as a wet dream."

"Mrs. Whitfield, is that likely? Ms. Appleyard is not a virgin. Just hours previously she had been made love to by your son. She described this event to me this morning as unlike any such she had ever experienced in her life, in that . . ."

"In that what?"

"In that she felt totally consumed. After the event she was exhausted. She was uncontrollably hungry."

"Nevertheless, Dr. MacBride, if I understand you

correctly, Joan reported this to you, her confidential psychiatrist, as a dream." Lacey stressed the word *confidential.*

"Even if it was only a dream, as you suggest, Mrs. Whitfield, your nephew provoked it."

"What?"

"There remains the question of responsibility."

"Are you saying . . . ?" Shades of Dot Palmer's New Age philosophy. Shades of Dot Palmer's new age. "Oh, my dear. Well, I thank you very much for forewarning me." Lacey took the phone away from her ear and mouth. "And forearming me."

Lacey disconnected.

Lacey Calder Whitfield had been socially significant all her life. She was well used to the multifarious ways people use to insinuate themselves into the lives of the socially significant. Bearing bad tidings regarding her friends, brother, husband, children, magnifying something way out of proportion, outright lying, offering synthetic insights, clucking sympathetically was only one approach. One of the worst.

All else being the same, would Dr. MacBride have called Lacey Whitfield, as she just had, if Lacey Whitfield were a single mother on welfare?

She thought not.

The phone was still in her hand.

She slid the sleep mask up onto her forehead. On the phone she punched #B.

"Obadiah?"

"Yes, Mrs. Whitfield?"

"Everything going all right for the party? The caterers doing everything correctly? The place for the musicians to play arranged?"

"Yes, Mrs. Whitfield."

"Obadiah, do you happen to know where my nephew Skylar is at the moment?"

"He and Ginny went out in a canoe. They took a picnic. They've been gone hours."

"I see. When they arrive home, call me. Then give me ten minutes. Then bring Skylar to me. Bring us tea."

"Yes, Mrs. Whitfield."

Lacey put the receiver back on its cradle.

Skylar on the river, camping for lunch in the woods somewhere, with her thirteen-year-old daughter . . .

She replaced the sleep mask over her eyes.

One thing about having a family, Lacey said again to herself, is that it's deucedly difficult ever to have a nap.

On the country club's terrace overlooking the tennis courts, Jon borrowed a chair from another table and slid it to the table where his sister Calder sat with Tom Palmer, Jr., his mother, Dot Palmer, and Jonesy.

There were used salad plates before them, half-empty glasses of iced tea before Dot and Jonesy, empty glasses of gin and tonic before Calder and Tom.

Terri Ainsley also sat at the table, but not at a set place, a glass of orange juice in her hand.

They did not interrupt their conversation to greet him.

". . . very attractive," Calder said. "Like something you'd see in a zoo."

"And leave there," Tom said.

Dot said, "He even smells vaguely like . . ."

"A zoo," Calder said.

Jon noticed Jonesy's eyes became momentarily intense.

He asked Calder, "How did you and Tom do?"

"Very badly," Calder said. "We've both been playing this course all our lives. It is so annoying to have people come in from Maine and Long Island, who have never played this course before, and beat us at it."

"I suspect you're bored with it," Dot Palmer said.

Jon looked at Tom's empty gin and tonic glass. "We're playing doubles in a few minutes."

"Yes." Tom handed his glass to a passing waiter. "I'll have another."

Calder giggled.

Jon asked Jonesy, "You all right?"

Jonesy jumped slightly. "Why do you ask?"

"I suspect you all were talking about cousin Skylar. I feel guilty, running out, leaving him at home." Jon remembered the night in Tennessee Skylar had taken him to the Holler. His "club." A roadhouse.

"I don't," Calder said.

"I wish you had brought him," Terri said. "I'm looking forward to meeting him."

"I forgot," Jon said. "You're going to go to Knightsbridge School of Music, too, aren't you, Terri? You'll get to meet him tonight."

"Piano," Tom said. "Terri actually gets to manipulate eighty-eight notes. And several chords. She gets to use both hands. How many notes has a trumpet?"

"What a stupid thing to say," Jon said.

Calder asked Jon, "When are you delivering Skylar to his digs in town?"

"Tomorrow afternoon."

"Not this afternoon?"

"What do you mean?"

"Get rid of him. Before hundreds of people show up at our house. You actually want a cousin standing on one leg while he scratches his tick bites on the other, asking people 'How's your cows'?"

"That's not very nice of you."

Tom said, "He's embarrassing."

Jonesy said, "I really think you ought to, Jonathan. Bring him intown, I mean. Make some excuse."

"What? Why?"

"I don't like him," Jonesy said. "I have my reasons."

"Actually," Jon said, "he's much more subdued here than he is at home. Less high-spirited."

Jonesy said, "He smolders."

"At home in Tennessee he knows everybody, how everything works. He'd never met a stranger. I was disoriented when I went south. I misread things, places, people. Think how disoriented he must feel."

"He smolders." Jonesy took a deep breath. "He exudes."

Jon said, "Here he doesn't even slip into his cracked English much. His dialect. His rebel's dialect. Did you ever realize that 'hisself' makes more grammatical sense than 'himself'?"

Calder said, "Oh, come off it, Jon. You boys did a certain amount of bonding while you were south, yuk, yuk, yuk. This is the beginning of a new century. America. Your bubba Skylar is still a slave to ideas, social structures we abandoned decades ago. What does he talk to an ambassador about? Drums! Native drums! Everybody here is trying to sell electronic infrastructure to the ambassador's country, and Skylar yaks it up with him about drums! Embarrassing? Oh, yes."

"Hey, he's your cousin. He's family."

"Since when has that mattered?" Calder asked. "I don't want him in my family."

"You don't owe your families anything," Dot Palmer said. "You don't owe your parents anything. That proposition has been perpetuated generation after generation just to retain the status quo: the supremacy of the white male."

Tom smiled appreciatively at his mother.

Quietly, Jon asked, "Not to keep us in touch with our own culture?"

"There's a difference?" Dot asked. "You're all individuals. You have your rights. Be in touch with yourselves. Do as you feel. If you don't like Skylar, get rid of him."

"Don't you like him?" Jon asked Dot Palmer. "Do you find him absolutely objectionable?"

"Oh, I find him charming," Dot said. "Attractive, in a rustic sort of way. But you all seem to have some negative intuition about him. Isn't intuition the only truth there is?"

Looking at Dot Palmer, Jon realized again that, although fifty, she recently had been made a full professor at a college down the road that had managed to remain mostly for women. He said nothing.

"Stop thinking there is some moral imperative," Dot said. "There is no such authority, natural or supernatural. Have your schools taught you nothing? Jon seems stuck on the fact that Skylar is your cousin. Facts mean nothing. You find him annoying. You don't have to deal with him, you know. Just get rid of him."

Slowly, Jon said, "For one thing, I don't think the police would like to see Skylar Whitfield disappear down the road just yet."

"Ah, yes. The jewels. Does the possibility that Skylar has your mother's jewels affect your feelings toward him?" She was grinning widely.

"What jewels?" Terri asked.

"Some of Mother's jewels went missing during the night," Calder told her.

"Are they valuable?"

"Yeah. I guess you could say that."

"You think Skylar stole them?" Terri asked.

"He was," Tom intoned, "the new element in the house."

"I hope he did steal them," Dot said. "It might be a most intelligent and instantaneous response to his new and unfamiliar situation. His way of showing contempt for you brats."

"Skylar's not a criminal," Jon said.

"Are you sure?" Dot asked. "Lacey has told me Skylar's girlfriend was murdered this summer."

Terri asked, "His girlfriend was murdered?"

"And," Dot continued, "that Skylar satisfied the court of his innocence." Beaming at Jon, she said, "Shall we take the time to deconstruct the facts as Skylar manipulated them?"

"Come on, Tom," Jon said. "It must be time for us to win men's doubles."

"You don't know Skylar is not a criminal, Jonathan," Dot said. "The most you can say is that you feel he isn't. Or perhaps you really feel he is?"

Standing up, Tom gulped the rest of his gin and tonic.

Jon muttered, "Somehow I feel we're not going to win anything this way. And that's a fact."

Chapter 9

"Let's just try our best to get through tonight," Wayne said to his brother-in-law, Vance Calder.

In the cobblestoned driveway of Paxton Landing Vance opened the driver's door of his Porsche.

"We'll meet with Lacey tomorrow afternoon," Wayne said, as if he had not said it before. "Maybe later, the kids. I don't know."

Climbing into his car, Vance asked, "What time?"

"I don't care. Two-thirty. Three. Whenever everybody has recuperated from the party tonight."

Vance's face was tight. "Okay."

Slowly, he drove his Porsche over the cobblestones toward the road.

"Where's Skylar?" Lacey asked.

Obadiah wheeled the tea tray between the small upholstered chairs in the small sitting room adjoining Lacey's and her husband's bedrooms.

"He's gone to get a shirt, Ma'am."

"Ah! Being polite, is he?"

"After being on the river, I think he finds the house rather cold."

"I should have known better."

Skylar stood in the open door. On his T-shirt was some art blob, without doubt publicizing a rock band or some such thing. Years before, Lacey had ceased trying to decipher such blobs.

She said to Skylar, "You look like a big streak of sunlight standing there. Come in! I thought you and I would have tea, just the two of us."

Skylar looked at the serving tray. "Hot tea?"

"Of course."

"I don't believe I've ever met anyone before who actually drinks tea when it's hot."

"You've never had hot tea?"

"No, ma'am."

"It's why we waste the money on air-conditioning, Skylar: so we can waste more money drinking our tea hot."

"That's a beautiful gown, Aunt Lacey. Is that what you're wearing tonight?"

"This is a dressing gown, Skylar."

"You mean, you wear that gown while you're getting dressed in another gown?"

Lacey laughed. "It doesn't make much sense, does it? I suppose not much about us does make sense to you. Sit down, Skylar."

Soundlessly leaving, Obadiah closed the door behind him.

"I didn't take the time to shower," Skylar said. "Mr. Obadiah said you wanted to see me right away. But Ginny and I did jump in the river before heading back."

"How do you like our river?"

"Weird. No snakes."

"The river is too polluted for snakes."

Handing Skylar a cup of tea, Lacey said, "Skylar, I've been meaning to ask you. How are your parents?"

Since he'd been there a full day, the question surprised Skylar as much as hot tea on Labor Day weekend. "They're just fine."

"Tell me about them."

"Well, Dad sells insurance, all lines. Mama works in the public library. Together, we've worked to keep the farm going, at least enough to pay for itself. Mostly cattle. A little tobacco."

"You were brought up on the same farm my husband was."

"Yes, ma'am."

"Try a sandwich. Cucumber."

Their crusts removed, the sandwiches had been quartered. Skylar helped himself to six quarters.

"Odd," Lacey mused, "that in twenty years or whatever, I've never met your parents. My in-laws."

"My parents have never traveled much."

I have, Lacey thought. I've even been through the Nashville and Memphis airports, more than once.

I never even thought of calling them.

Neither did Wayne, apparently.

"Or been to the farm where my husband was raised."

"People say it's a pretty place."

"We've exchanged cards at Christmas," Lacey said.

"Yes, ma'am."

"Sometimes even photographs."

"Yes."

"And how's your friend Dufus?"

"Dufus is Dufus," Skylar said. "Always has been. Always will be."

"I was sorry to hear about your personal tragedy this summer, Skylar. That your girlfriend was . . ."

"Murdered."

"Yes. Were you very much in love with her?"

"We were friends."

"But not lovers, I take it." Skylar did not respond. "You like girls, of course."

"Some of them."

"I mean . . . Well, have you ever been in trouble with girls?"

"Sure enough. Plenty of times."

"Really? Tell me."

"Well, there was the time Tandy was bounced off her horse and couldn't help rollin' down the slope and ended up hangin' on to a rotten tree branch over a right sharp drop. We had some trouble that day, I'll tell you."

"Who's Tandy?"

"Tandy McJane. This girl I grew up with? And then, once we went into a cave to get out of a right big storm, thunderin' and light'nin' to raise the saints, and after we got into the cave we discovered there was this big nest of rattlesnakes between ourselves and the way out of the cave we hadn't noticed when we went in? And—"

"I mean, have you ever gotten a girl in trouble?"

"Gotten a few out of trouble. Tandy's gotten me out of trouble, too, plenty of times. There was the time she helped me escape the jailhouse—"

"You haven't gotten a girl pregnant?"

"No, ma'am. When you're brought up on a horse and cattle farm, there's not a whole lot of ignorance about how such things happen. I mean, sometimes all sides of you critturs are fornicatin'—"

"Have any young women ever accused you of being, shall we say, too forward?"

"Forward?" An image entered Skylar's mind. He blushed.

"That's not what I mean, Skylar. Perhaps I should say, accused you of being too bullish? Of forcing yourself on a girl?"

"Now why would I have to do that? What would be the pleasure in it? No, ma'am. Sometimes . . ."

"Sometimes what?"

Skylar swallowed hard. "I don't know what to say. We're talkin' about sex?"

"Trying to."

"I thought you might want to talk to me about your missing gembobs."

"No, Skylar. I don't think they'd look well on you."

"Force?" Skylar frowned. "Tell the truth, ma'am, sometimes a girl and I have come at each other pretty strong. Isn't that all right? Tandy's always game. Mrs. Duffy taught me that there are two most important things about lovemakin'. The first is to know what you want; the second is to know what your partner wants; of the two, the second is the more important. That's the best way to pleasure both."

"How very odd," Lacey said. "I remember my husband once saying exactly that. Who is Mrs. Duffy?"

"She runs a roadhouse called the Holler. Your husband knew her."

"I think I'm learning more than I want to know. More sandwiches?"

"No, thank you, ma'am."

"I see. And tell me again, who is this Tandy? Is she the girl who . . ."

"Was murdered? No, ma'am. That was another girl."

"Are you trying to confuse me?"

"I'm not trying, ma'am."

"What do you think of Miss Appleyard?"

"Who's Miss Appleyard?"

"Jonesy."

"Her name's not Jones?"

"Joan Appleyard."

"Jon Than's girlfriend."

"Yes. Is that how you think of her?"

"Yes."

"Quite attractive, isn't she?"

"I suppose."

"I noticed the two of you out on the terrace last night together. After dinner."

"For a few minutes. Then I went to Jon's room. Called my parents. I called them collect, by the way."

"No need to call collect, Skylar. We never see our phone bills."

"I mean to call 'em again shortly. This is the first time they've been without me."

"You saw Jonesy later, didn't you? During the night?"

"No, ma'am. I went to bed. I was tired from the long bus ride."

"Why did she leave Paxton Landing so early this morning?"

"How would I know?"

"I see," Lacey said, because nothing else to say came to mind. Was it possible that during the night, Jonathan . . .

"Ma'am? I've been answering your questions, questions I ordinarily wouldn't answer, bordering as they do upon the private, you might say, because you're my aunt, and I've come here to school, and for the first time am away from my parents, and maybe you and Uncle Wayne feel you have some responsibility for me and ought to get to know what I'm like, probably fearful I might raise some kind of hell, and, truth be told, some folks think of me as a bit of a hell-raiser, but I'm just a good ol' boy, I'd no more think of stealin' your gembobs than I'd think of tryin' to herd geese—"

Lacey raised her hand. "I'm sorry, Skylar. You're quite right. I couldn't have stated it better myself. You're a gracious young man. I'm sorry if I've embarrassed you."

Skylar grinned broadly. "Sex doesn't embarrass me, ma'am. Maybe talkin' about it does, with a woman who I guess hasn't spent much time in the pasture, even if you are my aunt—"

"How did you like your hot tea?"

"The sandwiches were real tasty." Skylar, knowing himself excused, stood up. "It sure would take a bunch of 'em, though, to get me and Dufus through a day of makin' hay."

"I daresay. Go call your parents, Skylar. And be sure and give them my best."

"Aunt Lacey sends her best to you all," Skylar said into the phone.

"Hey, Skylar!" his father, Dan Whitfield, answered. "How're ya doin'?"

"You picked up on the first ring."

"I'm at my home desk, on a Labor Day Saturday evenin', tryin' to arrange some insurance for the new owner of the Sinclair farm."

"Who bought it?"

"You mean, what bought it? Some kind of a corporation, calls itself, let me see, Repo, Inc."

"Someone mean to store repossessed cars on the place?" The Sinclair place was an antebellum farm not far from the Whitfield Farm. "It's gettin' real hard to preserve the South, isn't it? We might just have to rebel again."

"I've been told to insure it as a working farm."

"That's good. How's Dufus doin'?"

"Haven't seen much of Dufus since you left, son. Had to do a couple of hours of fence-mendin' this morning. Dufus was nowhere in sight."

Monica, Skylar's mother, came on the phone. "Honest, Skylar, I do believe that boy is trying to drink up all the beer in Greendowns County by himself."

"He can do it. He's not drivin' my truck, is he?"

"I don't know how he's gettin' around," Dan said. "So how is Lacey?"

"She don't mind talkin' about sex."

"Oh?" Dan said quickly.

"Aunt Lacey had some of her gembobs stolen from the house last night."

"Her jewelry?" Monica asked.

"Much?" Dan asked.

"Yeah. From a safe in the downstairs study. The police have been here."

"Burglars?" Dan asked.

"Some think I done did it," Skylar said.

"You gettin' along all right with your cousins now, Skylar?" Dan asked.

"Fine. That Ginny's a fine filly. A bit spraddle-legged yet, but I suspect she knows where the green grass is."

"She's the thirteen-year-old," Monica said. "How about Calder?"

"Calder needs her ears pulled down," Skylar said.

The bedroom door opened. Jon entered, still dressed in tennis whites.

"You and Jonathan gettin' along all right, Skylar?" Dan asked.

"I haven't had to whup him again. So far." Skylar smiled at Jon. "Guess once you whup that boy, he stays whupped. We're doin' fine, Jon Than and I are. Even sleepin' in the same room together. I'm tryin' to teach him to keep his feet under the covers, so old Slick don't grab his soul."

Jon smiled. "Say hello to your folks for me."

"He says hello."

"I thought he must be with you, way you were talkin'," Dan said. "Saw Reverend Baker this morning. Says we'll sure miss your trumpet playin' in church tomorrow mornin'."

"Skylar," Monica said. "I think maybe you should talk with Tandy. She misses you, you know."

"I'm just doin' as she told me to," Skylar said. "She and Jimmy Bob still circlin' each other?"

"The wedding is planned for two Saturdays from now," Monica said. "She's draggin' around."

"It's true," Dan said. "She's not walkin' the same. Instead of lookin' like she's leadin' a band, she looks like she's pullin' a cartload of sand."

"Uphill," Monica added.

"Reason I called," Skylar said, "is to give you all the number of the phone where I'll be in Boston tomorrow night. This rooming house Jon Than has arranged for me."

"Go ahead," Dan said.

Skylar recited the number. "Same area code. Got to get goin'. These here Whitfields have invited a few hundred of their best friends to come visit tonight."

"Isn't that nice," Monica said. "They want to show you off."

"Sure," Skylar said. "Bye."

Sitting on the edge of his bed, Jon had removed his tennis shoes and socks. "It's ninety-two degrees out," he said. "Dad said Mr. Lowenstein is delivering some clothes he wants you and me to wear tonight. Has he been here yet?"

"Not as far as I know."

Jon yawned. "You showered?"

"Yeah."

"Skylar, I'm sorry I ran off on you today. I had to go to the club. Play in the tennis tournaments."

"You win?"

"Singles. I thought you'd be bored with our so-called friends." Skylar didn't say anything. "What did you do, alone all day?"

"I haven't been alone. Ginny had a picnic made up. We spent the day exploring the river in a canoe."

"Oh. I've never done that with Ginny."

"And your mama gave me tea. Hot tea. And a fistful of sandwiches."

"Really? Where?"

"In that little sitting room outside her bedroom."

"I've never had tea with my mother, like that."

"I've had a fine day," Skylar said. "Didn't realize you were gone till Ginny happened to mention it."

Jon headed for the shower.

"Yes, sir," Skylar told him. "I found all kinds of good places to hide gembobs, I did."

Chapter 10

"Oh, goody," Skylar heard his aunt Lacey mutter. "Here comes the Alex Broadbent flotilla. As if we couldn't have done without him. And them."

Skylar looked at his watch. It was nine-fourteen.

To him, it seemed the evening had been going on hours and hours. More than one night. Almost all his life.

While Jon was in the shower there was a rapid little knock on the bedroom door.

With only a towel around his waist, Skylar opened the door.

Three well-dressed people entered—a portly man in his fifties, a lithe man in his early thirties, and a woman less than thirty.

"You must be Skylar Whitfield," the portly man said.

"I must," Skylar agreed.

"I'm David Lowenstein. Tailor. We have your party

clothes for you. Do I hear Jonathan in the shower?"

The younger man carried two plastic zip-up suit bags.

"Have you showered and shaved? Excellent! We'll dress you first. We haven't much time. Also, we are terribly eager to see how these clothes work." The three were surveying Skylar's body as if, it seemed to Skylar, he were a field to be sown. "Yes!" Hands on Skylar's shoulders, Mr. Lowenstein said, "I think we have things exactly right!"

Glancing at the woman, Lowenstein suggested to Skylar, "Why not slip your underpants on before you remove your towel?"

"Right." Skylar swallowed hard. "Why not?"

He did so.

"We designers for years have been trying to come up with formal wear using shorts, because shorts are what men usually wear now, isn't it?" Mr. Lowenstein rubbed his hands together as he watched Skylar. "Or should I say, aren't they? Which is right? So much more comfortable, practical. Dancing and all. I'm so rattled. This is very exciting!"

"Exciting . . . ?"

Lowenstein held out what appeared to be just a short-sleeved shirt. Except that across the shoulders, down the back and three quarters of the way down the sleeves the cotton cloth took on the appearance of a formal jacket. Attached to the front of the shirt were lapels. The sides of the shirt, under the arms, were tapered, white. Between the lapels the white shirt was ruffled.

Mr. Lowenstein buttoned it up for him.

"Fits perfectly!" Mr. Lowenstein clapped his hands. "Looks wonderful! I do believe we've done it!"

With bright eyes and wide grins, his assistants agreed joyfully.

The woman held out the black shorts for Skylar to step into. Under the circumstances, shaking slightly, he found doing so a great deal more difficult than mounting a tall horse.

"It's never made any sense, has it, for men to wear shorts, and then a long-sleeved shirt and a long-sleeved coat on top? Now has it?" Mr. Lowenstein ran his hands over Skylar. "I may have designed the perfect solution! That looks tremendous!"

Towel around his waist, Jon came out of the bathroom.

He said, "Looks nice."

Skylar asked him, "Jon Than, why is this happening?"

"Oh, Jonathan." Again Mr. Lowenstein rubbed his hands together. "Do you like it?"

Still looking at his cousin, Jon said, "Yeah."

"Finally I have designed something that will make me famous!" To Skylar, he said, "White socks, please, to bring the ensemble together!" He raised his index finger. "Black tie!"

While Skylar stood aside, doing nothing about socks or tie, the dressing process was repeated with Jon, with the same joyful oohs and aahs, same laying-on of hands. Except that Jon watched the process in his full-length mirror.

The night before, Jon had supplied Skylar with formal shoes, socks. And tied his bow tie for him.

Grinning, Jon glanced at Skylar through the mirror. "Embarrassed, Skylar?"

"Damned right," he muttered.

Mr. Lowenstein gave Skylar a surprised, hurt look. "Why?"

Skylar said, "People just don't behave this way at Wal-Mart."

Mr. Lowenstein laughed. "That's a good one!"

The assistants gathered up the plastic and pins.

"Hurry down, young gentlemen!" Mr. Lowenstein said at the door. "We want to get some good photographs of you. It will mean a lot to us to have your pictures in the morning newspapers." He raised his arms. "A revolution in men's clothing! By Lowenstein!"

After the door closed behind them, Jon flapped his arms around. "Wow. Comfortable. You look cool, Skylar."

"I'm burnin' up."

"Why?"

"I feel like a woman! Jon Than, no one's ever dressed me since my diapers fell off and I was put out into the sideyard to grow up!"

"Not fun for you? Cool clothes!"

"That guy's hands were all over me!"

"Sure."

"What do you mean, 'sure'? If your daddy hadn't happened to mention his name to me I would have slapped him sideways till Sunday."

"Skylar." Jon was tying his own tie. "Mr. Lowenstein has four children. His father and grandfather have done tailoring for the Calder family for as many generations. He's a friend. Got it? He's designed these clothes. It's important to him that we wear them, and appreciate it. This is a big thing for him."

Jon took another black tie off his bureau and put it around Skylar's neck.

"I feel like a jackass on mule day."

"Don't you usually?"

"No. I don't."

"Hold your chin up, damnit!" Jon had to stand behind Skylar to tie the black tie. "Bend your knees!"

"You Yankees sure relate to each other funny."

"Why do you say that?"

"You sure take a pawin' lightly!"

"Skylar, haven't you caught on yet that nowadays men are sex objects, too? Live with it."

"Not me, babe."

"So what if people 'paw' us? Some people. Servants, barbers, tailors, teachers, coaches. I guess it is one way we relate to each other. It means nothing. Maybe a little affection, approval. I don't know. Anyway, it's not what you think it is. Only time you lay hands on anyone, Skylar, is when you're lovin' a girl or whuppin' a boy. Isn't that true?"

Skylar tugged the two sides of his bow tie.

"You're all a bunch of girls," Skylar muttered.

Photographers, T.V. feature cameras awaited them downstairs.

Mr. Lowenstein shepherded Skylar and Jon, Jonesy, and two other girls in short party dresses down the stairs, through the front hall, into a living room, onto a terrace while people shot their cameras at them.

"You're Skylar," a girl said to him. "I'm Terri Ainsley. I'll be going to Knightsbridge with you. Piano. Why do you look so mad?"

"I feel like a damned doll."

"You are a doll." Raising one foot behind her, she kissed him on the lips.

Skylar took her in his arms, and kissed her hard.

"Damn!" she said.

"Sorry." Skylar wiped her lipstick off his mouth. "Just felt like bein' myself there for a minute."

"Anytime," Terri said.

From then on, Jon dragged Skylar everywhere, indoors and onto the terraces, making a point of introducing him to every person. "I want you to meet my cousin Skylar Whitfield from Greendowns County, Tennessee. Skylar's come north to study the trumpet at Knightsbridge School of Music. You should hear him play!"

A string quartet played on a raised platform on the main terrace.

After several introductions, Skylar said, "Jon Than, will you please stop all this?"

"All what?"

"Walkin' me around with you. Both of us dressed this way, I feel like part of somethin' Preacher Baker warned me to consider twice before joinin'."

"No. Come on. There's someone over here I want you to meet."

Skylar met people who had Doctor, Judge, General, Admiral, Mayor, Governor, Congressperson, Senator, Professor, in front of their names; a huge number of people with corporations spoken just behind their names; two National Football League players, one retired hockey player, two male film/television stars, three female; two novelists, one poet; a duchess; a recent candidate for president of the United States, and one couple who owned a sixty-thousand-acre farm in Argentina.

Waiters circulated with silver plates of hors d'oeuvres.

Skylar was introduced to one couple named Nance. The lady was in a wheelchair.

"I believe you know my daughter," she said.

"Ma'am?"

"Louise Oglethorp. We live next door."

"Haven't actually met her," Skylar said.

"She speaks as if she knows you," Mrs. Nance said.

"Ginny must have told her a lot about you."

All the young people, except Terri, seemed to be attending Harvard, Yale, Princeton, Brown, Dartmouth or M.I.T.

"Jon Than, don't you folks know anyone either poor or stupid?"

"Guess not. Come on."

Almost all openly admired the cousins' fashionable clothes. The athletes in particular noted Mr. Lowenstein's business address.

After what seemed like hours of this circulating, after Skylar had met everyone, Jon said to him, "Skylar, you greeted all these people as if you really respect them."

"I do really respect them."

"Why?"

"They've taken on more responsibilities than others have. They've accomplished more than others. Don't you respect these people, Jon Than?"

"No. Not really."

"Why not?"

"Guess I wasn't brought up to respect people."

"Then how can you respect yourself?" Skylar grinned. "I mean, if you ever do accomplish anything that deserves respect?"

Jon wandered away.

Skylar got a beer from one of the several bar tables, and stood aside. He had raised eyebrows at the bar table by insisting he be given his beer still in its can.

After a glimpse of his uncle Wayne Whitfield early on, in a corner deep in conversation with Judge Ferris, Skylar had not otherwise seen him.

So far, Skylar had come within hand-shaking distance of Vance Calder and his big blond wife twice. He had been completely ignored by them.

There were other men at the party dressed formally in shorts. Mr. Lowenstein was right: They did look strange in shorts and long-sleeved jackets.

Not far from him, Calder and Tom stood with a group of other young people. They were all looking at Skylar.

Suddenly, they laughed in unison.

Skylar believed he saw all their teeth at once.

Now the waiters were carrying silver bowls and trays to several buffet tables.

Terri Ainsley looked over at Skylar from a group of older people. She smiled at him. With her left hand, she gave him a low wave.

Skylar smiled back.

Suddenly Jonesy was standing in front of Skylar. He had not seen her approach.

"Skylar, about this morning . . ."

He waited.

She stared at his shirtfront.

"What about this morning?"

"What happened between us?"

"This morning?"

"Last night?"

"Got me."

Skylar saw Ginny in a short, frilly pink party dress dodge her way through the crowd.

"At dinner?" Skylar asked.

"I mean . . ."

"On the terrace? Forget it. You're Jon Than's girlfriend. I guess you'd had more wine than I had." Skylar noticed that in the center of the terrace his aunt Lacey, while being talked to by a man with a beard and a great watch fob, was watching them. "We're supposed to be friends, you and I."

He started to move toward his aunt.

"That's not what I mean, Skylar."

"Sure it is."

As he approached his aunt, she turned to look at the terrace's entrances from the river.

She then muttered, "Oh, goody. Here comes the Alex Broadbent flotilla. As if we couldn't have done without him. And them."

Different-looking people were coming onto the terrace. Some of the men had hair as long as some of the women's; some of the women's heads were as bald as some of the men's. Some wore torn blue jeans and sneakers, one a Western shirt and boots, one, a frock coat with flowing black tie, one, a black suit with clerical collar, one, heavy chains padlocked around his neck, with a diaper pin through the lobe of his left ear. One woman wore a veiled black picture hat and a black gown that trailed behind her; another, pink hotpants and brown boots that rose just above her knees; another, a skirt, blouse, and sensible brown shoes.

Singly, they matriculated into the crowd.

Beer can in hand, alone, Skylar ambled off that terrace to a lower terrace nearer the swimming pool.

In the dark, away from the crowds, alone, he thought, Skylar took a deep breath. He touched his toes with his fingertips. He did a deep-knee bend. He took another deep breath.

He took a swallow of his beer.

He looked at the moon rising over the river.

"Ha, Skylar. How're ya doin'?"

The voice both startled and amazed him. It was deep and low and slow.

Skylar looked around in the dark. "Who . . . ?"

Something white, a shirt collar, rose in an arc from one end of a bench to its center, turned, became a shirtfront. Whoever he was, he had been lying flat on his back on a stone bench.

"Alex Broadbent," the low, deep voice said. "At your service."

"You're supposed to be on the upper terrace."

"Why?"

"You just arrived. Up there."

"Clearly not."

"How do you know me?"

"Ginny. She's told me all about you."

"Are you a man?"

"Distinctly. Undeniably. Irredeemably. Unapologetically. Happily. Why do you ask?"

"Sir. I'm not questioning your masculinity. Your voice . . ."

"Yes. *Ex cathedra.* I've been told about that. I gather it rather annoys some. I pause. People accuse me of reaching for dramatic effect. Some even accuse me of lecturing. Truth is . . ." A lighter flared. A cigarette was lit. ". . . I'm a closet asthmatic, trying to breathe."

"And you smoke?"

"Doctors prescribed cigarettes for me when I was a boy. I believe tobacco has saved my life, so far. Prevents sensitivity to allergies by gunking up tendrils or something, so I was told. I was told someday I'm going to choke to death anyway, no matter what. But that's enough about me. How are you enjoying your visit to New England?"

"I'm here to go to school."

"Knightsbridge. Trumpet. Composition."

"Was that music I heard last night coming from your place? It was real different."

"Different. Yes. A composition for strings one of our houseguests is working on. Did you enjoy it?"

"I couldn't hear it that well."

"Come down to my humble abode anytime, Skylar. You'll be most welcome."

"Why?"

"Because I believe you are trying to do something with sound. With time. Am I right?"

"I guess."

"I prefer such people to those just trying to do something with bills and coins, popularity and power."

"Ginny tells me you're powerful."

"How?"

"You write. You speak."

"I'm not powerful because I write, or speak. If I have any power at all, it is because I listen."

"So why aren't you with your friends up there, at the party?"

"They're working," Alex said, "to the slight annoyance of your aunt Lacey. Artists and the wealthy need each other. The arts do not exist in a vacuum. And they do not do well in a classless society. Artists need the wealthy, those with disposable income to support the arts. And the wealthy, who are apt to be, if not insular, insulated, need the artists, to instruct them in how it really is to live in a time and a place. Only together, really, do they record a culture." The tip of the cigarette glowed brighter. "Right now, I'd rather listen to you. So far, you haven't told me much."

"What do you want to know?"

"Where did you hide the gembobs?"

Skylar said nothing.

Alex laughed. "To use your own vernacular, right now you don't know whether to laugh, cry, or get your gun. Enough said. The eloquence of silence."

After a moment, Skylar said, "Guess I'll go back to the party. Aren't you hungry?"

"Skylar?" In midair the light of the cigarette disappeared. "You may have need of me. Don't hesitate to come to me. Okay?"

". . . Okay."

Chapter 11

"Hunker and tap, hunker and tap, then, wreck 'em!" Sweating, the ambassador was hugging Skylar around the shoulders with one strong arm. The ambassador's face was sweating, his eyes glassy. Skylar smelled good bourbon on the ambassador's breath. "My boy! The young man who knows more about diplomacy than two thirds of my colleagues at the U.N.!"

After dinner, the string quartet had been replaced by a six-piece dance band.

The band was taking its second break of the evening.

Skylar and Terri Ainsley had been dancing together continuously, enthusiastically, athletically, happily.

Most of the people who danced at the party did so as if totally bored. There were some good dancers, of course, especially among the older folks, the smoothies. There were others who tried but appeared to Skylar like whooping cranes trying their legs at a futile mating ritual.

Some of the people watched Skylar and Terri enviously, admiringly, lovingly. Others watched them through eyes hooded with contempt.

Swirling, two or three times Skylar noticed Jonesy watching them. The expression on her face was, to him, unfathomable.

"Should we stop?" Skylar asked Terri while they were dancing.

"Stop what? Havin' fun?"

"Some might think we're showin' out." He jerked his head at the world in general.

"To hell with them," Terri said. "They're the ones who are acting badly! This is a dance, not a stockholders' meeting."

Still clutching Skylar to him, the ambassador put his other arm around Terri and pulled her, too, to him. "Beautiful young people! For you, all the wars have been fought! Please, please appreciate it! Love each other!"

Outside the ambassador's tuxedo lapel, Skylar could see only one of Terri's brown eyes. It was warm and happy.

Skylar said, "Yes, sir!"

After the sound of the band, only soft conversation could be heard on the terrace.

"Come on!" Skylar took Terri's hand.

She skipped after him. "Where are we going?"

"I have an idea."

They went to Jon's room.

Skylar fastened Jon's kidney belt around his waist. Then he fastened all Jon's belts together. He looped one belt around the back of the kidney belt and fastened it.

For the first time since being at Paxton Landing, he took his trumpet out of its case.

"I'm going to play for the ambassador. Then we'll give them a laugh."

He explained to Terri what he wanted her to do.

She giggled. "Are you crazy?"

"You're supposed to entertain at a party, aren't you?"

"I don't know, Skylar . . ."

"Sure. It's only polite."

While the band was taking its break, many had gone to the bar table for new drinks.

Around the terrace there were many groups of from two to six people engaged in conversation: business, politics, the arts.

There were those selling themselves, or their ambitions, to others.

There were others listening cautiously, for the most part not buying, at least not immediately.

There was no more relaxed joy at this party than there would be at any convention of people, each with his separate agenda.

Suddenly, from over the guests' heads came the startlingly clear, pushing sound of a trumpet playing slowly a tune none there had ever heard before, a strong, simple, sweet tune that spoke of the depth, the solemnity, the joy, of real love, of lasting love.

Conversations stopped. People turned. They looked up.

Skylar sat on the railing of a dimly lit, second-story balcony, head down. He was addressing his horn as if he were adoring it.

The crowd remained speechless until Skylar, to make a phrase soar, eyes closed, raised his head and rotated it, sending his sound all over the people.

On the terrace, Lacey said, "My God!"

Elsewhere on the terrace, Tom Palmer said, "How crass!"

"Gross," Calder said.

Ten meters away, Judge Ferris said, "Charming. Absolutely charming!"

Wayne Whitfield stepped out from a door of the house and looked up. A smile played both sides of his mouth.

Jonesy said to herself, "Oh, my Lord!"

On the river side of the terrace, Alex Broadbent said, "Ah! Skylar has a flair for the theatrical."

Receiving no response but silence to his first selection, Skylar played a second, this one faster, jollier, with more of a carnival sound to it.

"The boy must be drunk!" Lacey said.

"Oh, it is beautiful!" Mid-terrace, hands clasped under his chin, the ambassador's face was raised to the balcony. Tears streamed down his cheeks. "So beautiful!"

"He's really showing off now, isn't he?" Dot Palmer, sitting alone, asked the air.

Calder found Jon. "Jonathan! Get him to stop this instant!"

"Why?" Jon asked.

"Because it's gross! Crass! Ugly! Repulsive!"

"Why?" Jon asked.

"What will he do next, strip to his G-string? Go shove him off the balcony."

It was just then that Skylar began playing the tune about the daring young man on the flying trapeze who flew through the air with the greatest of ease.

As a shadow, Terri appeared behind him.

And shoved Skylar off the balcony railing.

Most gasped. A few snorted in derision.

"Oh, my God!" Lacey screamed.

Without missing a beat, Skylar swung from the belts fastened to the balcony, not only playing the song but demonstrating it, as it were, his back straight, his legs straight, his head up.

A few laughed and applauded.

"Oh!" The ambassador released his gasp. "He is so beautiful!"

"Ah!" Alex Broadbent said. "Skylar has a talent for satire. He knows exactly how these people regard him. And I'll be damned if he isn't making fun of them!"

"Jonathan!" His mother's voice cracked like a whip five meters from Jon.

Jon began to amble toward the house.

By the time he reached the door, the trumpet had stopped playing. Skylar was scrambling up the balcony and over the railing.

The band was returning to its platform.

Full out, not much together, the band played "The Man on the Flying Trapeze."

Only two couples tried to dance to it.

"My belts?" Jon was grinning. "You used my belts?"

"Sorry, Jon Than. Didn't do 'em no harm, I reckon."

They had returned to the terrace.

Skylar had replaced his trumpet in its case in Jon's room.

When they entered the terrace some were smiling at Skylar; others scowling.

Many were leaving the party.

The ambassador had not only hugged Skylar with both arms but given him a wet kiss on his forehead. "Beautiful boy! You must come to my country!"

Skylar pushed him off, but laughed.

One lean man dressed in a straight, no-frills black-tie rig not only smiled at Skylar; he winked.

Instantly, not having really seen him in the dark of the lower terrace, Skylar knew that man to be Alex Broadbent.

Jon shrugged. "I never knew I had so many belts."

"You have a whole passel of belts, Jon Than. Good ones, too. I'm glad none of them broke."

"Interesting thought," Jon said. "What if one had? You'd be on your way to the hospital now with broken knees and ribs and a trumpet sticking all the way through your head."

"Anything for a laugh," Skylar said. "Seemed to me most of these folks here need somethin' closer to a laugh than a smirk."

"Oh. Is that why you did it?"

Looking into each other's eyes, the cousins smiled.

"Fox," Jon said.

Terri Ainsley appeared. She took the fingers of Skylar's right hand in her hands. "I have to go back to Cambridge with my parents now. Home."

"Oh," Skylar said. "Okay."

She kissed him on his cheek. "See you, Skylar?"

"Oh, yes."

Sliding his fingers between her palms, releasing them, keeping her eyes on his face, Terri said, "See you, Skylar."

"Oh, yes."

Jon smiled at him. "I do believe you've made a friend."

Skylar said, "She's fine."

Lacey joined them.

"I'll go see if I can find Jonesy," Jon said. "Last dance."

"What on earth did you think you were doing?" Skylar's aunt Lacey asked him.

"Entertainin' your friends, ma'am?"

"We were not entertained."

"Not?"

"If you want to act the clown, Skylar, please go join the circus. There are a great many people here of great talent and accomplishments. We do not ask or expect them to perform. Certainly I did not expect a drunken nephew to swing through the air over the heads of these truly accomplished people while playing a nursery tune on a toy instrument!"

Astonished, Skylar knew not what to say.

"How much have you had to drink, Skylar?"

"One whole beer, ma'am."

"Who helped you? Who pushed you off the balcony?"

Skylar did not answer. He noticed his aunt seemed to be wearing more than enough jewelry.

"If, and I say 'if,' you are ever invited to Paxton Landing again, young Skylar, please do not disturb our guests again by such a vulgar display of your dubious minor talents!"

She turned away from him.

Performing a charming face, she said her good nights to Alex Broadbent and a woman with him.

Expressionlessly, his uncle Wayne watched Skylar's face from an open door to the house.

"Skylar?" Jonesy slid her fingers between the buttons of his shirt and moved the backs of her fingers up and down his sweating skin as much as the buttons allowed.

Skylar said, "Jon Than's looking for you."

"I know."

"Last dance."

"Skylar? Can we go somewhere?"

"Where?"

"Somewhere we can make love again."

Skylar took a deep breath. " 'Make love again'?"

"Make love." Her eyes were glassy.

"Jonesy? I don't—"

"I want to fuck again."

"I don't understand you at all, at all. No, I don't."

"Skylar, you know what I mean. Don't lie to me."

"I have no more idea what you mean than an elephant lookin' at a piano, Ms. Jonesy."

"Oh, Skylar!" Lightly she hit his chest with the sides of her fist. "Don't be such a bastard!"

Wayne was watching them.

"You'd better take me, Skylar. And I mean it!"

Gently, he took her wrists. He lowered her hands to her sides. "Jon Than will be real disappointed if he doesn't find you, Jonesy," he said, "for the last dance."

Skylar caught up with the Broadbents at the top of the stairs to the lower terraces.

Skylar said to Alex, "Mind if I go home with you all now? Right now?"

Looking up at him from the steps, Alex smiled. "You in that much trouble, Skylar?"

"Yes, sir," Skylar said. "Yes, I am."

Alex said, "You're most welcome."

Chapter 12

Covers thrown off, the nude young woman writhed on her bed. Her legs were separated, stretched wide. Her fists, either side of her head, thrashed back and forth on the sheet. Her head tossed from side to side.

Her every muscle was taut.

The sweat drenching her body glistened in the moonlight coming through the window.

"No, no, no," she whimpered. Her hips began to quiver, undulate to an increasing beat. "Yes, yes, yes!"

Three-thirty in the morning, the moon had not set.

Having left the Broadbents' boathouse, full of music he had never heard before, visual arts the likes of which he had never seen before, conversation such as he had never heard before, humming, Skylar started up the slope to the main house of Paxton Landing.

From downriver of the boathouse there was the screech of car brakes. A tremendous bang. The loud sound of metal being crunched. Breaking glass. A woman's scream. Through the trees Skylar saw a flame shoot up for only a second. There was a splash.

Then silence.

Absolute silence.

Shocked, hands in his pockets, Skylar continued looking at the site a few seconds, wondering, assimilating what he had heard, seen.

Running toward the site he passed the front of the boathouse. He yelled, "Hey! Help! Hey!" as loudly as he could while running at full speed.

On the riverbank, at first he saw nothing.

Then he saw two rear car wheels upside down, half submerged in the river.

There was no one on the riverbank.

Not removing the light shoes he had borrowed from Jon, Skylar plunged into the river.

He stood beside the passenger door of the upside-down car.

Peering through the murky water he could see little. The car was a convertible with its top down.

He put his face below water.

A young woman's head was outside the door frame. Underwater, her hair and head moved in the river's current.

Skylar dived.

Reaching under the car frame, he grabbed the girl's shoulders and pulled. Only the top of her body moved, and that, not much. She was wearing a seat belt.

It took him three dives to release the belt. He had to swim under the car to its middle to release the catch.

He saw there was a young male in the driver's seat. He was wearing tuxedo trousers.

Each time he surfaced he gulped as much air as quickly as he could and dived quickly again.

Thank God for these clothes, Skylar thought. Thank God for Mr. Lowenstein's clothes. I never could be doing this in that monkey suit I wore last night.

At some point he realized the couple in the car were Tom Palmer and Calder Whitfield.

On the fourth dive he braced his feet against the car door and pulled Calder out.

He dragged her through the water. He placed her on her stomach, head down, on the riverbank. Straddling her, his knees either side of her on the ground, hands spread wide, pushing down hard, he pushed down on her back again and again.

After several pushes water splurted from her mouth.

Her vomit reeked of alcohol.

Shortly, she coughed.

She was breathing.

After only one or two more pushes, he let gravity do the rest.

He dove back into the water on the driver's side of the car.

Blood was in the water around Tom's head.

Skylar tugged at him without success. With his hands he felt for a seat belt. Tom was not wearing one.

The steering wheel was pressed against Tom's ribs.

Diving again and again, Skylar continued pushing Tom's big body, however he could grab it, toward the center of the car, out from under the collapsed steering column.

At first, the body would not move.

Surfacing for air, Skylar realized he was crying. He was about to lose Tom Palmer, if he hadn't already.

"Oh, God!" Skylar yelled at the sky. "Please!"

A few more tries, and Tom's body suddenly became free.

First grabbing Tom's left shoulder, then, with both hands, his head, Skylar pulled him out from under the car.

As quickly as he could, slipping and sliding, Skylar dragged him to shore. He placed him, too, head down on the riverbank.

Sobbing, Skylar pumped and pumped Tom's back.

Calder's head raised from the mud. Moonlight glistening in her eyes, she looked over at Skylar.

"Oh, Skylar," she said. "You damned bastard!"

"Please, please, please," Skylar chanted.

Suddenly a huge quantity of alcohol-reeking water began to pour from Tom's mouth.

"Yes!" Skylar continued his respiration until Tom's head rose.

Tom tried to throw Skylar off.

"What the hell you think you're doing?" Tom asked him.

"Saving your life, fool."

"Oh, my ribs hurt." His head fell to the ground.

The moon set. It suddenly became a very black night.

Skylar could not tell where the cut or cuts were on Tom's head.

Tom was passed out.

Calder was passed out.

Faster than he had ever run, falling once, Skylar dashed through the woods and across the lawn.

With the side of his fist, he banged on the solid front door of the Broadbent boathouse.

It seemed forever before the porch light came on and the door opened.

In a white cotton bathrobe, Alex looked out at Skylar. "Been swimming?"

"I need help. Tom Palmer and Calder had an accident. Their car landed upside down in the river."

"Did you get them out?"

"Yes. Pumped them out. They're both breathing. They've passed out."

"Good for you."

"Call the police. Rescue squad."

In the big living room two men and a woman slept on separate couches; one young man was in a sleeping bag on the floor.

Alex woke them up. "Quick," he said to them. "There's been an accident. Go with Skylar."

"Ambulances," Skylar said. He didn't know where the phone was.

While these people were putting on footwear, glancing at Skylar, Alex found a medical kit and two flashlights. He handed them out. "Go. Do what you can. I'll be right there."

"Will you call for ambulances?" Skylar asked. "I know Tom is hurt—"

"Where are they?"

Skylar told him.

"I'll be right there."

At a run, Skylar led the three men and a woman through the woods to the site of the accident.

In his kitchen, Alex picked up the phone and pressed a button. "Wayne? Alex here. Calder and Tom Palmer have had an accident. Skylar pulled them from the river. He says he's got them breathing now but they are unconscious."

"You haven't called the police, have you?" Wayne asked.

"No."

"Good. Don't. Where are they?"

Alex told him.

"I'll be right there."

Shivering as much from spent nerves as cold, Skylar sat on the ground next to a big tree. His nose was running.

Skylar guessed Tom had missed the curve and hit the big tree at an angle. The car had ignited, flipped over, and landed upside down in the river.

Tom must have been driving very fast.

Skylar wondered how there had been time to do all that he had done. Had he done things in the right order? Ought he to have pulled Tom out before giving artificial respiration to Calder?

It was a wonder they were alive. The impact of the accident. The fire. The water.

He had had so little time.

How had it been humanly possible for him to get to the scene of the accident, see enough in the moonlight, dive and dive and dive, release Calder's seat belt, force Tom out from under the steering wheel, pull them ashore, give them both artificial respiration before either drowned?

How had there been enough time for him to do all that?

His lips moving silently, Skylar said, over and over, "Thank you, Lord!"

His uncle Wayne had arrived with Obadiah and another big man. They brought more lights.

In Wayne's hand were some tools.

He crouched over Calder. "What happened?" he asked her. "You all right?"

"Oh, Dad." Calder was flat on her back. "That bastard. Skylar. He hurt me."

"Oh, is that what happened? You're pretty drunk, girl. Can you get up?" He asked Alex, "You think they can be moved?"

"Tom will have to be carried. I wish we had a stretcher. I'm pretty sure he has some broken ribs."

Wayne stood up. "We haven't got a stretcher. May we bring them to your house?"

"Sure."

"I asked Dr. Danforth to meet us there." He said to Calder, "Try to get up."

The woman helped Calder stand. "Oh, wow," Calder said. "My head. I'm sick."

Her knees buckled. The woman held her up.

"Seeing you're already wet," Wayne said to Skylar, "will you do me one more favor?"

Skylar did not answer.

Wayne handed him two pairs of pliers and a screwdriver. "Will you go take the license plate off the car? And everything out of the glove compartment? Everything else you can find? There'll be a tow truck here to dispose of the car in a few minutes."

Skylar did not have to dive to remove the license plate. Diving to remove things from inside the car, for the first time Skylar realized how bad the river water tasted.

By the time he was done, everyone was gone from the riverbank. They had taken their lights with them.

Big double headlights shining, a tow truck came along the old timber road. The road curved back to the main road this far from the boathouse.

Skylar waved the tow truck to stop. He pointed out to the driver the wheels in the river.

Then, still shivering, he walked quickly up the lawn

to the main house. He carried with him everything he had taken from the car.

There were many lights on in the boathouse.

The main house was dark and quiet. Skylar saw no sign of the big party there had been in that house only a few hours before.

Nor any sign the daughter of that house had been in a major accident less than an hour before.

Jon was in his bed, breathing deeply, asleep.

Skylar stripped off his wet clothes. He dropped them on the floor.

He crawled beneath his blankets. He was asleep before he had breathed thrice.

Chapter 13

Wayne Whitfield heard his brother's-in-law Porsche on the cobblestones of the driveway.

It was two-forty-five Sunday afternoon.

As Wayne moved through the house to his study, for some reason the house seemed to him particularly bright and airy.

Waiting, he looked through the window of his study into a small rose garden. He had had that garden planted so he could look out into it while working at his desk.

He could not remember ever sitting at his desk, actually looking out into that garden.

He enjoyed looking at it now.

Behind him, Vance Calder entered the room.

"Is Calder all right?"

"She will be," Wayne said. "Once she gets over one hell of a hangover."

"Is that what happened?"

"They were both drunk as skunks. We thought Tom had some broken ribs, but he's just sore. He's got a couple of cuts on his head which Doc Danforth sewed up for him. The Doc said Tom was so drunk there was no need for anesthesia."

"Where are they?"

"At the boathouse. Lacey's been down to see them."

Vance said, "I guess Skylar is quite the hero then."

"Calder's telling some drunken story about Skylar standing in the middle of the road and making Tom swerve, hit the tree. I haven't had a chance to talk to Skylar."

Lacey came into the study. "I can't find anybody."

"Jonathan's driving Skylar into Boston."

"Skylar's left? I must have been down at the boathouse. I never thanked him. I looked for him this morning. He wasn't in his bed."

Wayne closed the study door. "Skylar went to church this morning. With the maids."

"With the maids? My, my. I know where Calder is, of course. You know about the accident, Vance?"

"Wayne told me when I called this morning."

"Ginny's bed wasn't slept in, either. Did she spend the night at the Oglethorps'? I didn't get any such message."

"Ginny? I don't know."

Lacey sat in a wing-backed leather chair. "What's all this about? Why this meeting? Wayne? Vance?"

Wayne sat on a leather divan at the side of the room. He said nothing.

Vance, in his white trousers and striped summer coat, was the only one left standing in the room.

Finally, Wayne said, "I guess it's for Vance to tell you."

Lacey looked expectantly at her brother.

Vance said, "This is the hardest thing I've ever had to do in my life."

"What?" Lacey smiled. "After all your various divorces?" Her eyes then took fright. "This is something more major than divorce?"

"Lacey, as you know, I sold my yacht last week."

"Selling your yacht is more major than a divorce?"

"Vance," Wayne said, "I don't think that's the right place to start."

"We're bankrupt." Vance turned his back on his sister.

Lacey caught her breath. Her eyes grew wide. She shifted in her chair. "Who is bankrupt? You're bankrupt?"

"Calder Partners is bankrupt. My fault, I guess."

"That's not possible! Hundreds of millions of dollars . . . gone?"

"Gone."

"Over a billion dollars?"

"There wasn't that much, by June," Wayne said. "Nowhere near. As maybe you know, real estate had soured. Bonds had soured. All the safe investments have just been downturning. . . . Some of our investors had insisted we become involved as investors in the Commonwealth of Independent States. We did all the right things. People the other side of the old Iron Curtain seemed to pocket one dollar of every two we invested. So they perceive free enterprise. It was a while before we caught on to that."

"Still . . ." Lacey smoothed her silk dress on her thighs.

"Then Wayne had his heart trouble," Vance said.

"I knew you were under a lot of pressure," Lacey said to her husband. "I've been feeling so estranged from you, for so long. I felt you've been ignoring me."

Wayne shrugged. "I had worries. I guess you can say I worried myself sick."

"Why is this the first I'm hearing of it?" Lacey asked. "Of all this?"

Wayne said, "I wanted you all to enjoy your lives. I may have been wrong."

"Lacey." Vance turned to face his sister. "You insisted I leave Wayne alone. Refer nothing to him. Give him a chance to recuperate. You insisted I take sole responsibility for Calder Partners."

"Yes. I did. It was essential. Why not? It was high time you pulled your oar."

"I'd never run that damned partnership. Why do you suppose Father left Wayne as senior executive partner and not me?"

"Because you were off at your place in France getting married and unmarried like a starlet!" Lacey said with heat. "For a while there you had to have a motor yacht in the Mediterranean and a sailing yacht in the Caribbean!"

"No more," Vance said. "Both gone. And the place in Antibes will be sold as soon as I can get rid of it."

Lacey took a deep breath. She exhaled slowly. "What happened?"

"I made some bad investments. In some new financial instruments—"

"What investments?"

"They're called derivatives."

"Vance wasn't the only one skunked by them," Wayne said. "Other big boys were, too."

"Took some bad advice," Vance said.

"There are suits raging all over the country regarding these financial instruments," Wayne said.

"Do we get to sue someone?" Lacey asked.

"Can't afford to," Wayne said. "The loss is ours. And our investors'."

"Everything?" Lacey asked. "Hundreds of millions of dollars?"

Neither man said anything.

"Vance . . . Wayne . . . ?" Lacey looked from one to the other. "This isn't possible!"

Vance said, "It didn't take long."

Wayne said, "I sure did enjoy my rest, though. Never felt better physically. Pity my physical health has proven to be so expensive."

Lacey looked at her hands in her lap. "What do we do? The children . . ."

"The kids are fine," Wayne said. "Well off. As you must remember, I settled some of my own money on them, a few years ago. Out of my own earnings. Not Calder money. In separate trusts. No one, no creditors can get to those trusts." He smiled. "I forgot to settle any money on myself."

"The Calder money is gone?" Lacey asked. "All of it?"

Wayne stood up. "I think you'll agree with this, Lacey. Vance and I and Judge Ferris . . . and now, you . . . The Calder name has meant something, in New England, New York. So has the name Whitfield, I hope. We're known for our integrity, honesty, fairness—"

"Only recently, stupidity," Vance said.

"We could play bankruptcy games," Wayne said. "But I don't think your great-grandfather would want us to, or your grandfather, or your father. And I don't want to."

"Vance?"

"Nor I." He cleared his throat. "Of course. I may be stupid. I'm not dishonest."

Lacey said, "I know that."

"Thanks."

"We're of one opinion, with which I'm sure you agree, to cash in and settle up as well as is reasonable."

"What does this mean?" Lacey asked.

"To satisfy the creditors as well as we reasonably can," Vance said. "Everything with the Calder name on it goes."

"This house? Our home? Paxton Landing?"

"The kids are well off," Wayne said, "but they don't have the income to afford this house. To buy it from you. I sincerely doubt they would want to."

"Wayne, you can't get a job at this point. Not with your dickey heart. Everyone knows about it."

"Not much of a job anyway. Not after this. I'm not going to be able to buy Paxton Landing from you. I can't afford it either. The Calder homestead. Even if I could, it wouldn't look right."

"Oh, God." Lacey looked around the study. "My great-grandfather built this room."

"Yes." Wayne looked through the window into the rose garden. "He did."

"Why haven't you told me . . . ?"

Wayne said, "Thought we'd wait until after our traditional Labor Day party. You enjoyed it, didn't you? You always do."

"My hair . . ."

Wayne studied his wife. He would understand if she cracked wide open. "Looked great," he said.

"How much time do we have," she asked, "before all this breaks over our heads?"

"If it's all right with you," Wayne said, "we thought we'd make an announcement on Tuesday. What has happened. That we take responsibility for it. We will do everything possible to satisfy our creditors as soon as we can."

"And then what?" Lacey asked.

Vance said, "I'll give you fifty-to-one odds my wife will divorce me."

Chapter 14

After knocking quietly, Obadiah entered the study.

"There are three police persons here to see you." He looked at both Wayne and Lacey.

"More about the jewels." At the desk, Wayne's fingers twisted paper clips. "Why do they have to see us on a Sunday afternoon?"

Obadiah said, "They insist."

Vance had left the study a half hour earlier.

In the interim, Lacey and Wayne had remained in the study, talking, not talking. Wayne was trying to give his wife time to absorb, if not adjust to, as much as one reasonably could, the news she had just received. Her world, the earth and sky, the foundations of Lacey Calder Whitfield's life had just changed radically. Whatever good things and bad things there had been in Lacey Calder Whitfield's life, there had always been one constant: great wealth; all the social, psychological, financial security as real and apparently permanent as the sun around which all else revolved.

Her major question was: "Why didn't you tell me something of this before? Prepare us even a little for this disaster? I hadn't a clue."

After hesitating, Wayne had answered, "I think you can see why. I felt it was your brother who had to tell you. Undeniably, investing in derivatives was entirely his doing. It's taken a while for me to bring him around, get him to realize his mistake, as well as what his mistake means, to all of us. What would you all have thought of me if I had come, and—I hate to use a school yard term—told on him?"

"Oh, Wayne. You're still a Southern gentleman. Obeying some chivalric code."

"Maybe."

A heavy man in a suit entered the study, followed by two officers in police uniform, one male, one female. The female carried what might have been a large personal purse or a carryall of professional equipment.

"Mr. and Mrs Whitfield?"

Wayne rose from his chair. "Yes." He shook hands with all three. "You're not Lieutenant Cobb."

"You know Lieutenant Cobb?"

"He was here yesterday."

"Have you had a robbery?"

"You don't know that?"

"Isn't that why you're here?" Lacey asked.

"No, ma'am."

"Some of my jewelry was stolen."

"Sorry to hear that. Lieutenant John Cobb is in the robbery department. Burglary."

"And what department are you in?" Lacey asked.

"Mr. Whitfield, do you own a twenty-two pistol?"

"No. Well, yes." Wayne looked at his wife. "I gave such a thing to Mrs. Whitfield a few years ago when

I was traveling extensively on business."

"Where is it, ma'am?"

"Where it's always been. In the drawer of my bedside table."

"Do you keep it loaded?"

"Of course. What good would an unloaded gun do me in the event of an intruder in the middle of the night?"

"Not much. But you do have children in the house, don't you?"

"They don't know it's there. Why would they? How could they?"

"Would you mind if we all went to your bedroom to ascertain it is still there?"

"All of us?" Wayne asked.

"If you don't mind."

"Before we all go trooping through the house, I think you need to answer some questions first, Officer . . . ?"

"I'll explain all in good time. And I'm Lieutenant Hellman Forrest, two *l*'s, two *r*'s. Pleased to meet you."

Lacey rose from her chair. "I don't mind."

She led them all to her bedroom.

She opened the drawer in the little table beside her queen-size bed. "It's not here."

Lieutenant Forrest looked for himself. "No, ma'am. Is there anywhere else you could have put it?"

"No. I've never had it anywhere else."

"Have you ever carried it with you, in the house, or when you left the house?"

"No. Never. I thought it ridiculous when Wayne gave it to me. Except on Thursdays until midnight, there are always servants in the house, on the place. Our butler, the chauffeur. Well, the first week I had it, I took it outside two afternoons and fired it. At cardboard milk containers. Wayne showed me how to fire the gun the first afternoon. He told me to practice. I did. One other afternoon."

"When was that, ma'am?"

"Two or three years ago, when he began taking these longish trips to Russia, Ukraine. It's been in this drawer ever since. I doubt I've touched it since."

"Ma'am, when was the last time you noticed it was in the drawer?"

Lacey looked at the cold remedies in the drawer. "I guess last May, when I had a cold. I doubt I've opened this drawer since . . . since May." She closed the drawer. "Lieutenant, what is this about, please?"

"Your daughter Virginia?"

"Oh, no."

"Where is she, please?"

"What has happened to Ginny?"

"We're not sure anything has happened to her, ma'am. Do you know where she is right now?"

Lacey picked up her bedside phone. She pressed #B. "Obadiah, where is Ginny?"

"No one has seen her all day, Mrs. Whitfield. Mrs. Watts and the maids were talking about it at lunch. Her bed wasn't slept in. Apparently she did not come in for either breakfast or lunch."

"Perhaps she spent the night at the Oglethorps'. Didn't she leave a message saying so with anyone?"

"No, ma'am. Not the servants, anyway. Not you?"

"Thank you, Obadiah. If anyone sees her, inform me immediately." Replacing the receiver in its cradle, she said, "That's odd. Ginny has always been so good about letting us know where she is."

Lieutenant Forrest asked, "Would you show us her room, please?"

Wayne said, "Lieutenant, really! Mrs. Whitfield and I—"

"I know. You had a big party here last night. You do every Labor Day Saturday. You both must be tired. For now, please just do as I ask."

They all stood in Ginny's bedroom. Not a thing in the room was out of place.

"This is a kid's room?" Lieutenant Forrest said. "Everything so neat? My daughters could take a lesson. How old is Virginia, thirteen? Her own phone, computer, entertainment center. Wow." He opened one of the closet's double doors. "Mrs. Whitfield, can you tell what clothes might be missing?"

"No." Lacey looked into the closet. "Nothing seems to be missing."

"Those her suitcases on the shelf?"

"Yes."

"Her school knapsack on her desk? Her only one?"

"As far as I know."

"When did you last see her?"

"Last night. At the party. About ten-thirty, eleven. I assumed she went to bed."

"Was she alone when you saw her?"

"Yes. Honestly, Lieutenant, this is most provoking. I mean, worrisome."

"I'm sorry, ma'am. What was she wearing when you last saw her?"

"She was wearing a short, frilly pink party dress she didn't much care for. White shoes."

Lieutenant Forrest returned to the door to the corridor. "This robbery you had—when was it?"

"During Friday night," Lacey said.

"Tell me everything that was taken."

"Just some jewelry. From the safe in the study."

"Nothing else was taken?"

"Like what?" Lacey asked.

"I guess the gun in your bedside table could have been taken."

"I strongly doubt it. I was in that bed. If the burglar had gone through the house looking for things to take he would have found things of greater value than a cheap handgun. Other jewelry. There was other jewelry in my bedroom."

Forrest asked Wayne, "Do you have the serial number of the handgun you gave your wife written down anywhere?"

"No," Wayne said. "I'm sure not."

The female police officer took an air-locked plastic bag out of her carryall. In it was a .22 caliber pistol.

On the palm of her hand, without removing it from the bag, she held the handgun out to Lacey. "Could this be your gun?"

Lacey stared at it. "It could be. It certainly looks like it."

"You agree?" Forrest asked Wayne.

"I agree it could be. It's been years . . ."

"Now we need to sit down," Lieutenant Forrest said.

Lacey led the way back to the sitting room outside her and Wayne's bedrooms.

There were only two small chairs in that room, and a two-seater divan.

Lacey sat in one chair; Forrest in the other. Wayne sat in the middle of the divan.

The male officer stood by the closed door.

Lacey said, "I guess this is the day for my being sat down and told things I don't want to hear."

"Ma'am?"

"Never mind." Looking at her husband, Lacey's

face was drained of color. Her eyes were extremely pained. "Sorry," she said.

"We're going to play a tape for you." Forrest looked at the female officer. "This is the best way I know how to do this. I was called into the police station this morning. A local woman had arrived there with a story to tell. We taped her telling it. With her permission, of course."

The officer placed the tape recorder on a lamp table.

"To whom are we about to listen?"

"A Dr. Dorothy Palmer. She identifies herself as a professor at the college, a neighbor and longtime friend of this family. You do know her?"

"Yes. Very well."

The tape began by Dot Palmer identifying herself, by name, occupation, and address. She also stated the day and time (10:45 A.M.) the tape was made.

She continued: "This morning, a little later than usual because I had been at a party last night, I took my dog for a walk. On a leash.

"I was going along that wonderful low hedge in front of the Oglethorps' house when I saw a young girl, Ginny, Virginia Whitfield, standing alone on the lawn of the Oglethorps' house. She was on the lawn between that house and Paxton Landing, which is the property, the home of the Whitfield family. There is no doubt whatsoever in my mind it was Ginny. I have known her since she was born. And she knows me. I'm like an aunt to the Whitfield children. She was only fifty feet away from me. She was in full sunlight. I have excellent eyesight.

"She was still dressed in the pink party dress and white shoes I had seen her wear at the party the night before, which I thought odd.

"In her right hand was a gun.

"I called out to her. I said something like 'Ginny! Are you all right?' Yes. Those were my exact words.

"She looked at me a moment.

"Then she tossed the gun onto the ground.

"And she ran into the woods bordering the Whitfield property. I lost sight of her.

"I went back the few meters to the Oglethorps' driveway, entered their property, and went to about where Ginny had been standing on the lawn.

"On the ground was a handgun. I did not touch it.

"Rufus began to bark. He tugged at his leash.

"I followed him to the shade of the Oglethorps' great copper beech tree.

"On the ground I first saw skinny brown legs, arms. A striped blouse. White shorts, sneakers.

"Horrified, sickened I approached.

"Louise Oglethorp, whom I have also known since she was born, was in a most peculiar position, on her knees, hips leaning against the tree root, or base.

"Dry blood was in her hair at the back of her head.

"Clearly she was dead.

"It looked to me as if she had been executed, as one unfortunately sees in photographs of war, or Chinese prisons? Made to kneel and then shot through the back of her head.

"Again, I did not touch her. I came within five feet of her.

"Also, I did not raise an alarm at the Oglethorp house. I knew doing so would cause the scene of the murder to be disturbed.

"Instead, I jogged back to my own house. I didn't even put Rufus in the house. I put him in the car and immediately drove here to the police station.

"Which reminds me, Rufus is still in the car. What is the temperature outside?

"I suggested the police get to the scene of the crime as quickly as possible, before someone else stumbled across the body. Jilly won't, of course, as she is in a wheelchair. But her new husband, Edward Nance, who used to be a basketball coach, might. I frequently see him out and about when I walk the dog."

The tape turned a few more revolutions. There was a click.

Lacey said, "Excuse me."

She got up and went into her bedroom. She closed the door.

"Give us a few minutes," Wayne said to Lieutenant Forrest.

"Of course."

Wayne followed his wife.

The police remained in the sitting room nearly half an hour. Through the door, they heard the sound of vomiting, a toilet flushing several times, Lacey Whitfield sobbing, trying to talk while sobbing, Wayne Whitfield's deeper voice saying sentences they could not make out, some clearly repetitious, choking noises, the blowing of noses. . . .

The corridor door to the sitting room opened.

The butler wheeled in a tea cart. Without a word, Obadiah served each of the police a cup of tea and a plate of small cakes.

Just as quietly he left, leaving the tea cart.

"Sorry." Her face freshly washed, the front of her hair wet, Lacey reentered the sitting room. She went to the tea cart and poured her husband and herself cupsful. "I feel toward Louise as if she were my own child. She was always running about the place, in the game room, in the pool. Ginny and she were best friends.

Jilly Oglethorp, her mother, and I were at school together. Well, we were best friends, growing up. Still are, in most ways, I guess. My husband feels the same way."

The female police officer gave Lacey back her seat.

"Thank you," Lacey said. "This has been the most horrible shock."

"I'm sure," Lieutenant Forrest said. "I'm sorry."

From the divan, Wayne said, "I'm sure by now you've been to the scene of the . . . murder."

"Yes," Forrest said. "It was just as Professor Palmer described. Except . . ."

"What?" Wayne tried to suppress his impatience.

"It looks to us as if the young girl, Louise, was leaned against the base of the tree after she was murdered. There was no blood on the ground near her body, not that we've found so far. We believe she was murdered somewhere else and brought to the base of the copper beech tree. She was not shot through the back of the head, execution style. She was shot in the face, we believe from very short range. With a twenty-two caliber revolver."

"Enough," Lacey said. "Please."

After a moment, Forrest asked, "Have you any idea where Ginny is?"

Eyes closed, Lacey said, "No idea on God's earth. She is a very bright, inventive child. She could be anywhere."

"Had she any money of her own? I mean, cash?"

"Of course."

"How much would you say?"

"I have no idea."

"Could she have come back to the house this morning, after Dr. Palmer saw her, and changed clothes?"

"I doubt it. Not without someone seeing her. Ourselves. One of the servants. I didn't see her party dress anywhere in her room. Did you?" Lacey squeezed her eyes shut. "Lieutenant, am I inferring you think our daughter Ginny murdered Louise Oglethorp?"

"Has she many friends within walking, running distance?"

"Of course."

"Please, will you give us a list of their names, phone numbers?"

"Certainly. Although what would people think if Ginny showed up on Sunday morning wearing a party dress? They'd know something was wrong."

"We'll also need good photographs of Virginia," Forrest said in a low voice. "A good full-length picture, and a good head shot, if possible."

"Has news of this been on the radio, Lieutenant, or television?" Wayne asked.

"I think not. As far as I know, there has been no reference to this on the police radio. No reason for it to have been. I'll make sure there isn't." He glanced at the female police officer. "I called the coroner and forensics on my portable phone. The victim is a child, and . . ."

Wayne said, "You think the perpetrator is, too."

"And it is Sunday of Labor Day weekend. I expect the press is shorthanded today. We'll try our best to suppress this news, at least until we know more."

"We appreciate that."

Forcefully, Lacey said, "Lieutenant Forrest, there is one thing of which we all may be certain. Virginia did not kill Louise Oglethorp."

Forrest sighed. "Mrs. Whitfield, I want to believe that. I really do. But where did the gun come from, if not from your bedside table? And who else would have taken it, if not Ginny?"

Chapter 15

"Vance?" Hunched over his desk in his study, Wayne spoke into the phone. "Ginny seems to have disappeared. The police have just left."

" 'Seems to have disappeared'?" Vance's voice rose. "What does that mean? Ginny wouldn't run away. Why would Ginny run away? You mean Ginny has been kidnapped?"

Trying to prevent further burbling from his brother-in-law, which Wayne could not stand at this moment, he said flatly, "The little girl next door has been found murdered."

"Oh, God! Louise Oglethorp?"

"Yes."

"Oh, God, that sweet kid! How could this—"

"How could what?" Irritated, Wayne spoke sharply. "At this point, we don't know much."

"Did someone kill Louise Oglethorp and kidnap Ginny? Oh, God!"

"Vance! Please just listen!"

"Wayne, let me catch my breath! Please tell me what has happened!"

"We don't know what has happened. Can't you understand that? I'm calling to ask you not to mention anything to anybody about what you and Lacey and I were talking about a couple of hours ago. We may have to postpone the announcement. At this time, it is not well for people to think we are vulnerable, on our downers, as it were, at least until we know more about this situation."

"No. Of course not."

"I hate to say this, but I mean, do not even let your wife know our financial straits at this time."

"Definitely not." His voice lowered. "I was just about to pour a martini in the old girl and tell her."

"Hold off on that. And about Ginny."

"Yes. Okay."

Jon entered the study.

Wayne signaled his son to close the door behind him.

Jon did so and sat in one of the chairs in front of the desk.

"What about Lacey?" Vance asked. "She must be close to a nervous breakdown. Have you sent for a doctor?"

"She's a strong woman."

"Wayne, what are you going to do?"

"First thing, talk to Judge Ferris."

"Yes."

"My emotions . . . Ginny . . ." Wayne rubbed his eyes. "As we used to say in the South, right now I just want to get on my horse and ride off in all directions. I need objective advice. Judge Ferris . . ."

"I'll come right over. I'll be with Lacey as soon as I can get there."

"Right." Wayne broke the phone connection.

He looked at his son without saying anything.

"What's wrong?" Jon asked. "What's happened?"

"Listen." Wayne pressed Judge Ferris's phone number. He waited until the maid got the judge on the line.

"Yes, Wayne? How did your session with Lacey go? Is she in a state of complete collapse? I wouldn't blame her if she were."

"Judge, I'm calling about something else. The police have just been here."

"Good. They must have a lead on what happened to Lacey's jewelry."

"This morning, Dot Palmer, while walking her dog, saw Ginny on the lawn of the Oglethorps' place. She had a gun in her hand."

"Ginny did?"

"Yes. She was still dressed in her party dress from last night."

"What time was this?"

"Nine, nine-thirty, I'd say. Maybe ten. When Ginny saw Dot, she dropped the gun on the ground and ran. Investigating, Dot found the body of Louise Oglethorp, kneeling, leaning against a tree. She had been shot in the face."

"Ohhhh." Wayne had never heard such a heartbroken sound as the judge made. "Dead? Is little Louise dead?"

In his chair, wide-eyed, Jon drew up. His back pressed hard against the chair. He yelled, "No!"

Wayne said, "Louise is dead. Dot immediately jogged home, drove to the police station, and made a statement."

"She didn't call you? Lacey?"

"No."

"Give me a minute, Wayne. Let me understand. Essentially, Dot Palmer, this morning, saw Ginny, dressed as she was last night, on the Oglethorp lawn, with a gun in her hand, and nearby was the murdered body of the little Oglethorp girl?"

"Yes."

"And upon seeing the Palmer woman, Ginny dropped the gun and ran away?"

"And no one seems to have seen Ginny since, or know where she is now."

"Dot Palmer is a most peculiar woman. She fashions herself an intellectual, but she has no sense of history. Which leaves her a victim of every intellectual fad that comes along, as well as of a totally overbearing, unjustified certainty."

In his chair, Jon sat stiffly. His hands gripped the chair arms. He was hyperventilating.

"Sorry," the judge said. "I'm just rattling along like the old man I am. Needless to say, I'm terribly shocked too. No matter what is revealed ultimately to be the truth, this is a terrible tragedy. The little Oglethorp girl, Louise . . . her mother in a wheelchair. But at the moment there appears to be only one witness, Dot Palmer, connecting Ginny to the murder scene—"

"She's a very good witness, Judge. She acted very intelligently, touched nothing, did not raise an alarm at the Oglethorp house, went straight to the police, in person. Her statement is concise and as clear as a bell on a cold night."

"But besides Dot's statement, there is nothing else linking Ginny to this tragedy, is there?"

"Yes. The gun found at the scene, a twenty-two caliber pistol, most likely is the one I gave Lacey two or three years ago."

"Why do you say 'most likely'?"

"Because Lacey's gun is missing. The gun the police just showed us probably is the same."

"Where did Lacey keep the gun?"

"Her bedside table."

"So anyone could have access to it."

"Dot Palmer saw it in Ginny's hand."

"And no one knows where Ginny is now?"

"No."

"It may not be fair, especially when a child is involved, but running away does imply guilt—at least in the mind of the public."

"I suppose so."

"Poor Lacey! She's had a double dose today, hasn't she?"

Triple dose, Wayne thought. Calder was nearly drowned in a drunken car accident before dawn. With Dot Palmer's son. "It hasn't been one of our best days."

"What about you, Wayne? Your heart . . . ?"

"Don't worry about me."

"Are you taking your pills?"

"I haven't thought about it."

"Do so. Who else knows—about Ginny, I mean—at this point?"

"Jon is sitting in front of me, hearing this for the first time."

"What about the press? Have they got hold of this yet?"

"Lieutenant Hellmann Forrest thinks not. Apparently he took some precautions against referring to it on the police radio, whatever, because of the age of the victim."

"That's decent. I know Lieutenant Forrest. He is a decent man."

"Good."

"Well. For the moment, we have to set emotions aside and put on our thinking caps."

"Do we need a lawyer at this point?"

"Oh, yes. Absolutely. A criminal attorney. I'm sure I can get Hastings. I'll call him immediately."

"Randall Hastings?"

"Yes. I suspect he's spending this weekend out at his place on Martha's Vineyard."

"I can do that. I can call him."

"It would be better if the call came from me. The first call. Then I'll have him call you. With a little luck we can get him to Paxton Landing by this evening."

"Good."

"I'll call Hastings first, as a matter of protocol. But even more than a good attorney at this point, believe it or not, we need a great public relations expert."

"Are you serious?"

"Yes, 'fraid so. Tiresome though it is, dreadful for a judge to say, such cases as these are more often won and lost in the press than in the courtroom. This will be a jury trial, of course. The way this case is presented to the public from word one is more important than anything. I'll call Randy first, out of courtesy. Maybe there is some public relations person in particular he would prefer to work with. If not, I'll suggest Coyne Roberts."

"You know her?"

"More to the point, I suspect she knows me. Wayne, do you have any doubt in your mind that Ginny did not murder her friend?"

Looking at the tears on Jon's cheeks, Wayne hesitated. "They had a rivalry, those two girls. From the age of three, they've been threatening to commit mayhem on each other. The way best friends do sometimes. You know? It all meant nothing, I'm sure. But I'm also sure people can be found, servants, whoever, who have heard Ginny threatening Louise, countless times. And Louise threatening Ginny."

"Have they ever before actually done bodily harm to each other?"

"Hair-pulling. They'd have fights and then make up, like any kids."

Jon was having great difficulty breathing. A sob escaped him. His father, the desk, were blurred behind tears.

"Wayne," Judge Ferris said, "it occurs to me this is not a very good time for you to announce the impending bankruptcy of Calder Partners."

"No."

"Sorry. I forgot Jonathan is with you. Jonathan does not know about Calder Partners yet?"

"No. He just returned from driving Skylar to town."

"Do you want me to call Vance and recommend he say nothing to anybody regarding Calder Partners at this time?"

"I've already done that. He's on his way here. I'm afraid I was rather sharp with him."

"In general, you have every reason to be. Vance is the slowest-witted Calder in known history." The judge paused. "The first thing, of course, is to find Ginny. Make sure she's all right."

"Lacey's working on that. So are the police."

"When you find Ginny, or she turns up, which I suppose is the more likely event, do not allow the police to know you have her; do not bring her to the police. If the police find her first, do not let them talk with her. Not one word. I would prefer that even you and Lacey do not question her until Randall Hastings and Coyne Roberts get there—if that's possible for you."

"I doubt that would be possible for us."

"I understand that. Do you understand I'm telling you to harbor a fugitive from justice?"

"Yes. No problem."

"I didn't think it would be. Just don't ever say that particular instruction came from me. I think I'll send a psychiatrist to Paxton Landing, too."

"We'll be fine."

"A child psychiatrist. At least have some such on immediate call. We may need expert testimony on Ginny's state of mind when she shows up."

"I see."

"I'm sure Randy will be able to advise me as to whom we should ask. Is Jonathan still in the room with you?"

"Yes."

"Turn on the speaker phone, please."

Wayne pushed the orange button on his consol. The phone's tone changed.

"Jonathan? This is Judge Ferris."

Wet-faced and dry-mouthed, Jon said, "Yes, sir?"

"This is a terrible tragedy. I cannot promise you, your father or your mother, your sisters, at this point, that things will work out well." The judge paused. Jon could say nothing. "I do promise you, however, that several of us shall do our loving utmost to make the very best of what seems at the moment very bad indeed."

Jon tried to answer.

The phone went dead.

* * *

After a moment, Wayne said to his son, "Jonathan, we've got to maintain our composure. Stay cool. See this thing through."

"How's your ticker?"

Wayne rubbed his chest. "Still ticking, thank you."

"Is there something else wrong? Something I don't know about? I thought I heard—"

"Nothing you need to know right now. I suppose you know about Calder and Tom Palmer?"

"Yeah. I met Skylar at lunch. I suggested we go for a swim before I drove him intown." Jon smiled through his tears. "He said he'd already been for a swim today."

"Indeed he had."

"Dad, I want to go back intown and get Skylar. Bring him back here."

"Why on earth would you do that?"

Jon surprised himself by saying, "Because he's a member of the family?"

"He's almost a complete stranger to us."

"Not to me. He's pretty good at things like this. Damned good. He ran from the law, too. Hid in the woods. He probably knows what Ginny is feeling, maybe how she thinks right now better than anybody. He knows how to hunt, to track." Jon swallowed hard. "I think he loves Ginny."

"He doesn't know this world at all, Jon. Not even the geography. He's as foreign to this world as a cougar to the arctic. He doesn't know how things work here, how people think here. He may love Ginny, but Ginny has a completely different set of experiences from Skylar's."

"He's very good with people. The ambassador fell in love with him."

"Proving they're both foreigners to this little world of ours."

"I think he ought to know."

"No. Definitely not. Jon, it is essential we manage the news of this event, as we discover it. Skylar handled the accident this morning properly, but—"

"But what?"

"Southerners . . ."

"You're afraid Skylar would talk."

"Yes. We must keep a lid clamped on this until we get some advice, know what we're doing. We just don't want a loose cannon out there—"

"You don't seriously think Skylar took Mother's jewelry, do you?"

"Jon, at the moment nothing is further from my mind."

"Okay."

"Besides: Be fair to Skylar. He's just moved from an isolated farm in the South to a major city in the North. He's matriculating at Knightsbridge School of Music in the morning. These are pretty exciting days for him. They ought to be happy days. We're strangers to him, too. Why should we distract him from the fun of all that with our problems?"

"You're thinking of that stupid trick he played last night, swinging from the balcony while playing his horn."

Blankly, Wayne said: "Skylar is not one of us."

"Okay." Jon closed his eyes. "What should I do? What can I do?"

"Go for a run. That's what I'd do, if I could. A long, long run."

Chapter 16

Jon opened the door to his parents' second-floor sitting room.

Telephone books in her lap, Lacey sat in one of the two small armchairs, talking on the telephone.

Jon sat in the matching chair.

"Mrs. Oglethorp, please. This is Mrs. Whitfield." Mother and son read the grief and fear in each other's faces. "Oh, Jilly, this is Lacey. I don't need to tell you how terribly, terribly upset and sorry we all are."

Jon also saw a touch of anger in his mother's face.

Jilly Oglethorp, sounding exhausted, said, "You needn't tell me, Lacey dear. I know you are."

"I loved Louise so. We all did."

"I know. I wouldn't have answered the phone to anyone but you. I know you are hurting as much as I am."

"Dear, you have no doubt in your mind, have you, that Ginny did not do this horrible thing?"

"Of course she didn't. I can't imagine what happened. I'm trying to think. Could it have been some madman you had at your party last night? Someone who worked for your caterer?"

"I sincerely hope not. Although the police have taken a copy of my invitation list. I'm sure they will check out the catering service."

"Was it one of those strange people who hang around Alex Broadbent? I mean, they are creative types. God knows what such are thinking and feeling and apt to do. The way some of them dress! I sincerely doubt dear Alex vets them all before bringing them out here."

"Oh, dear, we just don't know. This police Lieutenant Hellman Forrest, who called upon us and seems to be in charge of things, seems very competent. Sensible."

"Yes. He's upstairs now with his people investigating Louise's room. Although I don't know why. Surely the crime didn't take place there. . . . Lacey? This is very hard."

"I know, dear."

"Forgive me. I just can't talk to you anymore right now."

"I understand. Anything you want or need we can do—"

"We'll just have to hold hands through this, Lacey. The way we did when that big hurricane hit when we were little children. Remember how terrified we were?"

"I remember."

"Good-bye."

After clicking off the phone, Lacey looked at her son. Sitting in his shorts and tennis shirt he looked so clean, healthy, alive. How could someone even younger than he be so suddenly, violently dead?

Lacey said, "Do we need to talk now?"

"No," Jon said. "I guess not."

"I'm not ready for consolation yet, are you? It's all just too shocking. Overwhelming. Have you any idea where Ginny might be?"

"I guess since I've been at Harvard I've sort of lost track of Ginny. Her pals. Except for Louise, of course. I saw as much of her as I did of Ginny. Her comings and goings." Chin in hand, Jon stared at the carpet. "Have you any idea what I can do?"

"Stay alive," his mother answered. "Be alive. Why don't you go for a good, long run? Or swim laps or something."

"That's what Dad said."

"I guess you should stay out of the way of the police. Be polite to them, but . . ."

"Gotcha."

In his own room, Jon changed to running shorts and sneakers.

Then he ran miles along the paths behind the estates up the river to the highway over the bridge and, without stopping, he ran back.

Clear-voiced, not sounding a bit troubled, Dot Palmer answered the phone on the first ring. "Hello? Who is this?"

"Dot, this is Lacey."

"Lacey?"

"The police are here, coming and going. At the moment someone is in Ginny's room trying to establish her fingerprints or something." Dot said nothing. "They played us the tape you made this morning at the police station. I guess it doesn't leave me many questions to ask you." Dot still said nothing. "Dot, why didn't you call me?"

"It's a police matter."

"Is that all you have to say?"

"I'm not sure we should be talking to each other even now, Lacey."

"Dot, we've known each other for years. We've always talked. About everything. Louise is dead. You said you feel about Louise and Ginny as if they were your nieces. Essentially, you've accused Ginny of murdering Louise."

"I did not. I told the police what I saw. Precisely what I saw."

"You gave us no warning. Suddenly the police were here with this horrid news. Still you haven't called or come over."

"These things happen, Lacey."

"What do you mean by that?"

"These girls have been rivals, at each other's throats, all their lives. We all know that. You Calder-Whitfields never took it seriously. You thought it funny. Something was bound to happen."

"Are you saying you actually think Ginny may have killed Louise?"

"I know what I saw."

"Oh, Dot."

"You Calder-Whitfields have always had the attitude that no matter what happens, your money, your social position can handle anything."

"You're putting it to me—?"

"I'm not putting anything to you, Lacey. In this world, no people are better than any other, no person is better than any other, no idea is better than any other."

"How is that relevant?"

"What if it did happen as we all think it happened?"

" 'We all' who?"

"I've been trying to teach young people that the only truth is in their own feelings. They must realize themselves, do as they feel."

"Commit murder, if they feel like it?"

"If that's who they are. You're behind the times, my girl: still under the thumb of your father, Vance, Wayne, the oppressive white male who wants to control all via the Western Judeo-Christian-Islamic culture-with-a-K, contrived ideas of good and evil."

"I am sorry, Dot. I forgot you're so much cleverer than the rest of us."

Dot Palmer had only begun getting her degrees at age thirty-five, after winning a handsome divorce settlement from a husband she had made nearly suicidal.

After the divorce, Thomas Palmer, Sr., a certified public accountant, had gone to England and become an Anglican priest.

Lacey continued, "I don't have your degrees, of course, but what you are saying, my dear, strikes me as totally nihilistic."

"Don't use words you don't understand, Lacey."

Lacey took a deep breath. "Dot, do you know that this morning, before dawn, your son, Tom, dead drunk, had an accident? With my daughter Calder in the car with him? That he hit a tree on the old river road at high speed? That his car was thrown upside down deep in the river with both of them unconscious in it?"

Dot giggled. "Oh, is that where he's been?"

"You think that's funny?"

"Well, I guess Tom and Calder wanted to get drunk and go for a drive. How do we know what they meant by it? Calder was drunk, too, wasn't she?"

"Professor Palmer, now are you suggesting existential despair? I rather think it suggests careless, self-indulgent—"

"Are they all right?"

"If Skylar had not happened along to rescue them, they both would have drowned. They very nearly did."

"But they didn't."

"Skylar—"

"Skylar is a churchified, hypocritical, Southern, male pig."

"Skylar is a pig?"

"Where's Tom now?"

"Sleeping it off at Broadbents'. A few cuts on his face needed to be sewn up. Wayne got the doctor out. And had the car towed off. Needless to say, the matter was not reported to the police."

"Why not?"

"These young people have their lives ahead of them! Thanks to Skylar Whitfield."

"Lacey, you're not connecting one incident with the other, are you? The accident this morning, and my reporting on Ginny?"

"I don't know what I am saying. I am sick, grieving, confused. There is something called the social contract. Or do I dare use such a term with you?"

Dot laughed again. "You don't expect me to think in a linear fashion, do you?"

"Whatever I once expected of you, my dear, I'm not getting. But I will say that you are enough to drive anyone into the priesthood of the Church of England!"

Lacey clicked off her phone.

She shook her head.

She felt calling Dot Palmer had been a mistake.

She had accomplished nothing other than making herself more disgusted.

From her lap, she picked up Ginny's personal telephone book.

Trying very hard to keep her voice neutral, she telephoned every number in Ginny's book, asking if anyone had seen Ginny, or knew where she was.

None answered affirmatively.

Jonesy was stretched out on a long chair in the sun beside the swimming pool at Paxton Landing when the pool phone buzzed in its little box. At first she didn't care to answer it.

As she had seen none but the Whitfield servants all day, she finally reasoned the call most likely was for her.

Slowly she got up from the long chair and opened the telephone box and took up the receiver. "Yes?"

"Ms. Appleyard?" Obadiah's voice.

"Yes."

A click. "Joan? Is that you?" Dr. MacBride's voice.

"Yes."

"Joan, I've been so worried about you. I'm glad you came to see me yesterday morning. How are you feeling?"

"It happened again."

"What happened?"

"You know."

"That what's-his-name, the cousin, Skylar?"

"Yes."

"Oh, my God! When?"

"Last night. This morning. While I was in bed."

"Oh, no. Did he hurt you?"

"I'm exhausted. Absolutely exhausted. I've never

felt so worn out. I've spent most of the day in bed. My muscles—"

"Describe to me exactly what happened."

"The same as the night before. Only more so. I feel nauseous. I've been shaking a little. So I came out to sit in the sun. I'm still shaking."

"Didn't you lock your door?"

"There are no locks on the bedroom doors here at Paxton."

"I should say that gives the Whitfields a certain liability."

"For what?"

"Rape. They're liable for having someone like that in their house. I called Jon's mother yesterday and told her what you said—"

"You did?"

"I had to. They're responsible for having someone like that in their home. Wouldn't you say? Apparently she did nothing about it! She seemed very doubting, and hostile."

"She knew about it? She said nothing to me."

"Did nothing at all. Joan, you must do something."

"What?"

"How many hours ago was this?"

"Twelve? I don't know."

"Do you have any bruises on you? Any tearing in that area? Did you bleed?"

"I'm just exhausted. Shaking."

"Where is this Skylar now?"

"I don't know. Jon was supposed to bring him intown this afternoon. Boston. I suppose he's in Boston."

"Well, we're not going to let that boy get away with what he's done to you."

"He's done something to me, all right."

"Joan, you must go to the police. Report this matter to them. File charges."

"There were no witnesses."

"There seldom are in rape cases."

"Are you still in Wellfleet?"

"Yes. I'm sorry. I should be with you. I'm not due to return to Cambridge until tomorrow afternoon."

"May I give the police your phone number there? What is it?"

"I'll call them. We're about to leave for a clambake. You'll have to report it to the local police. Then I suppose they'll have to be in touch with the Boston police. I'll call the local police up there when I return from the clambake. I'll tell them you talked to me about this yesterday morning. Oh, dear. We should have done something about this yesterday. I shouldn't have passed responsibility on to Jon's mother. She seemed most uppity. Why did you stay at Paxton Landing last night?"

"I don't know. I've always felt safe here."

"You've been in a state of shock, my dear."

"Yes."

"There's no shame to being raped, Joan. I think I can safely say the police now take this matter seriously and sympathetically. If they don't, let me know. We'll land on them like a nuclear bomb." "I don't know."

"Do this, Joan. Do this now. Not only to put this boy where he belongs, in jail, but for the sake of your own mental health. Do you understand me?"

"Yes."

"I've got to run now."

"Thanks for calling."

* * *

"I feel like such a fraud." Phone books, including Ginny's, were on the floor at Lacey's feet. Her tear-soaked handkerchief was balled in her left hand. She spoke to her brother, Vance, who sat in the sitting-room chair Jon had vacated. "The dreadful news you and Wayne gave me a few hours ago. Now that seems like days ago. Calder and Tom, the car accident, dead drunk. What's the matter with them? Louise dead. Oh, where is Ginny? I've called everyone! Why doesn't she come home . . . ?"

"A fraud?" Vance asked.

"Yes. Queening at the party last night. With my wealth, perfect brother, husband, children, friends, home: I guess I always have. I didn't know how much was wrong. I guess I never did."

Lacey repeated, "A fraud."

When Jon came to the bottom of Whitfield's back lawn, he stopped running. As usual after a run, he began to walk up the back lawn, breathing deeply.

What he had been focusing on during his run was Ginny's pink party dress and white shoes.

Where could a thirteen-year-old girl go dressed that way during Labor Day weekend Sunday without being spotted?

As he ran, Jon found himself making up a Skylar-like metaphor: Dressed that way, Ginny should have been spotted as easily as a horned toad in a condom factory; whatever a horned toad is; whatever a condom factory looks like.

At an angle to Jon, Calder, barefoot, dressed in a

man's bathrobe, was staggering up the lawn toward the main house.

Tom Palmer, in wrinkled, bloodstained dress shirt and trousers, stood at the base of the steps to the boathouse. He blinked around him in the sunlight. His forehead was bandaged.

Falling to her knees on the lawn, Calder dry-retched.

Jon ambled over to her.

Tom said, "Where's my car?"

"You don't have a car anymore," Jon said.

"What did they do with it?"

"Scrapped it, I guess. You made a bad choice of car wash."

"Oh, Jon," Calder said.

He helped her up.

Tom said, "Mother hasn't finished paying for it yet. The car." Jon said nothing. "It should be my decision whether to scrap it!" He was annoyed.

"It was," Jon said. "You did."

Tom blinked at him. "Did what?"

"Scrap it."

Holding her arm, Jon guided Calder up the lawn. "Guess you guys had quite an adventure," he said.

"That bastard."

"Tom? Yeah."

"Skylar."

"What about Skylar?"

"Bastard."

"Skylar's a bastard?"

"What was he doing there?"

"Where?"

"In the middle of the road like that?"

"Skylar was in the middle of the road?"

"Oh, never mind. Get me into my own bed. I need . . ."

"What? What do you need?"

"I don't know."

Jon put Calder into her own bed.

After showering, he went to Ginny's room.

On her computer, he found a listing of names, addresses, telephone numbers of her friends and acquaintances, which he printed out.

There were school essays under various headings.

There was an incomplete draft of a love letter to Alex Broadbent, which began, "Dear Mr. Broadbent . . ." It was full of references to moonlight, rose petals, and, symphony orchestras.

There was a more-or-less daily journal. It was filled with venomous references to "Louise Uglythorpe," her latest victory over Ginny in schoolwork or sports, really quite witty descriptions of the violence and mayhem she would like to wreak upon Louise . . . which Jon erased. It seemed to Jon there had been no events in Ginny's life that had not been overshadowed by her perception that Louise had done better at them.

There was also what appeared to be an attempt at writing a short story. One girl did another girl, her friend, a "grievous injury," not specified. Forever, as long as they had known each other, this girl had been doing "grievous injuries" to her friend.

The two girls were standing on a narrow railroad bridge. A train was coming . . .

Jon erased that, too.

In his own room, Jon began calling down the list of Ginny's friends and acquaintances. Most who answered said Mrs. Whitfield had already called; many asked if something was wrong.

"Oh, nothing," Jon said. "Someone is here who wants to see her."

Chapter 17

Three flights down, the phone was ringing.

Except for the landlady, Mrs. Fitz, who had welcomed Skylar and Jon to the rooming house on Marly Street and shown Skylar his room on the fourth floor, the house seemed empty on this Labor Day weekend late Sunday afternoon.

After Jon had left, saying to Skylar, "I expect these digs are only temporary. After you find some friends, you'll probably want to make other living arrangements," Skylar had left the door to his very hot room open.

He had been putting his few clothes in the sticky bureau's drawers and wardrobe.

The phone kept ringing.

Finally, shirtless and in shorts, Skylar bounded down the three flights of stairs.

In the marble-floored foyer of the mansion, which obviously had been built as a family home, Skylar picked up the phone receiver. "Hello?"

"May I speak with Skylar Whitfield, please?"

"Uncle Wayne?"

"Skylar?"

"Yes, sir."

"Skylar, I thought you'd be interested to know Lieutenant Cobb just called me. He tells me they have a suspect in the robbery of your aunt Lacey's jewels."

"Have they recovered the gembobs?"

"No. They have discovered that one of the caterer's helpers, one who worked here Friday morning, helping to set things up, jumped bail in Minnesota last February on a robbery charge. At the moment they are not able to find the suspect, and believe she has fled."

" 'She'? A lady burglar?"

"A woman burglar. She didn't show up for work on Saturday. She's disappeared. Her roommate doesn't know where she might have gone."

"Do you believe it? How would she have known of the gembobs? You said she was at the house Friday morning. I understood the gembobs weren't in the house until you brought them home Friday evening."

"She might have heard talk. The servants here saying something about a security guard coming home with me, and why. . . ."

"How would she know of the safe?"

"A safe in a study wall isn't so unusual. The servants might have mentioned the security guard would be spending the night in the study, something like that. I thought you'd like to know you're no longer number one on the police's list of suspects."

"Aw, shucks. I knew my being number one at anything couldn't last."

"Sounds like this person needs to be arrested anyway. Be returned to Minnesota for prosecution."

"I sure would like for Aunt Lacey to get her gembobs back."

"Skylar? I have a something I must ask you. Precisely where were you when the car accident happened this morning?"

"Where was I? I had left the boathouse and was about fifteen, twenty meters up the lawn heading for your house, the big house. I heard the crash. Turned around. Saw a flame through the trees. Then a splash. Uncle, I ran like someone who had just put his baseball through a stained-glass window. I shouted at the Broadbents' house as I ran past—"

"You were not on that timber road? I mean, when the accident happened?"

"I was on the lawn between the Broadbents' boathouse and your house." Skylar repeated. "I was fixin' to pile into bed. It had been one night too long by half already. I didn't know that timber road was there until I ran on it tryin' to find the accident."

"Okay."

"Why are you asking?"

"One other thing. I expect it's tough being a silent hero, unsung. I wouldn't know, from personal experience, of course. You haven't told anyone about the accident this morning?"

"Jon. I haven't seen anyone else to tell."

"Good. Needless to say, your aunt Lacey and I are very, very grateful to you, Skylar, very obliged to you indeed, for acting as quickly and intelligently as you did. You saved Calder's life. To us, you'll always be a hero. And don't forget that."

"Ah just saw my duty and dood it. Be glad the moon was out. Otherwise—"

"But we ask you not to tell anyone about the accident. We didn't report the accident to the police. Do you understand? That's why I asked you to strip the car of its license plate and papers. That car has already been compacted. By the way, thanks for leaving those things in the study for me. Tom Palmer and Calder made a stupid mistake driving drunk, a mistake I'm sure they'll never make again. As long as no one else was hurt in the accident and there was no property damage, except the car itself—"

"And the tree."

"They . . . Tom . . . doesn't need this sort of thing on his record. He's got a good job at a brokerage house. Calder doesn't need—"

"I hear you."

"I mean, the less of such incidents people know of us, the better off we are, right?"

"Shoot, Uncle Wayne, where you and I come from people are downright proud of how many times they can roll a truck and live to tell about it."

"Not here. The less people have on you . . ."

"You suppose that's why you're all so tight-lipped, miserable neurotic?"

"What?"

"I won't even tell my bedpost that that ass pimple, Tom Palmer, just about killed my cousin Calder and ought to be put under the jailhouse for good and all. No, sir, not if you ask me not to. Howsoever, sir, I do suggest you keep that boy treed and never let me find out which tree he is in. If you understand?"

"Okay, Skylar."

" 'Cause if I ever discover just which tree that boy is in, I just might shoot his tail off for the sheer pleasure of seein' him fall down that tree ass-less, flappin' his arms, headfirst onto a standin' root."

For a moment, Wayne said nothing. Then he sighed. He said, "Thanks again, Skylar,"

And hung up.

After hanging up, Skylar looked up the three flights of stairs. He thought how hot it was up there in his room, just under the roof. Up there also was a horrible screeching noise he could not identify.

The house was totally silent. Skylar assumed Mrs. Fitz lived behind the curtained glass doors off the foyer in what had once been the mansion's living room.

The house smelled vaguely of dried mice.

He looked through the sworled glass windows of the front door into Marly Street. Across the road was another house similar to the one in which he stood. Lots and lots of similar houses, all sharing common side walls. He wondered if all those houses had been built at the same time. How could they build houses one after the other with common walls?

What do people do in cities on hot summer afternoons? To be outdoors? To be cool?

What do people do in cities?

Skylar opened the front door and sat on the front steps of the house.

It took him a while to discover the source of all the horrible screeching he was hearing. On the top of each house were metal ventilators. As the breeze turned them, each screeched a different note. As the breeze increased and decreased, each ventilator's screech raised and lowered on the scale and in volume.

He looked at the sweat on his forearms and thighs.

How come there was a breeze at the top of the buildings but not on the street?

How could people stand that screeching?

The noise was making him feel slightly sick in the head and stomach.

Did those ventilators make those awful noises all

the time? Why did people permit it? Did no one hear the screeching but him?

He came to Boston for music and found himself sitting on a hot stoop hearing worse screechings made by Man than he had ever, ever heard, even for a moment, in Nature.

"Stop a moment, Clarence. Just look at that, will you?"

The police car had been traveling along Marly Street at a crawl. Cars were parked both sides of the road. The two lanes in the middle of the road were lightly traveled this Sunday afternoon.

"What?" Clarence stopped the patrol car close to parked cars on the right-hand side of the road.

"If that isn't a chicken waitin' to be ate."

"That boy on the stoop?"

"Sittin' all tanned and muscular and slim, all shoulders and knees, near as naked . . . gleamin' in the sunlight like a roasted chicken just comin' out of the oven. He's a beautiful sight to behold, and I daresay he has no sense of what he is doin' at all."

"What is he doin'?"

"Insultin' the rest of us."

"I doubt he thinks that."

"If I wanted to see such a sight I'd go either to a beach or a museum, not to downtown Boston on a Sunday afternoon."

"He looks perfectly natural to me."

"Since when is it recommended to be natural?"

"Why don't you take him home, Bernard, for one of your five unmarried daughters?"

"Altogether, they wouldn't know what to do with him. His hair's not greasy."

"These days, Bernard, dressed that way, sittin' there, is not against the law."

"It's criminal," Bernard said. "Go along, Clarence, but let's you and I keep our eyes on that lad. He'll come to no good, I can tell you that."

On the stoop, Skylar heard the telephone in the house ringing again.

Again he tried to ignore it. He couldn't be the only one in the world, the city, Mrs. Fitz's house to relate to that phone.

More driven by the screeching of the ventilators than drawn by the ringing of the phone, Skylar went inside and answered it. "Hello?"

"Skylar? That you, Skylar?"

"TANDY!"

"Hydy, Skylar! You missin' me at all?"

"Not a bit! No, ma'am, not one bit!"

"Now say that ain't so, Skylar. How come you're not missin' me?"

" 'Cause you told me not to, Tandy, and I always do what you tells."

"How you like livin' in Yankeeland, Skylar? Is it real cold up yonder?"

"Real hot. Muggy like I never felt it. The wet heat makes my bones all rubbery."

"How you like those there Yankees, Skylar?"

"They all seem to be in some kind of agony."

"That's good. Well, you better get used to 'em. Guess you'll be there awhile. Also, looks like we're gettin' some Yankee neighbors down here. Your daddy said they're from Delaware, folks who bought the Sinclair farm."

"What's their name?"

"Repo. I guess their name is Repo. What kind of outlandish name is that? Isn't Delaware in Yankeeland?"

"You askin' me what Della wore?"

"Hush your mouth, Skylar."

"It's good to hear your voice."

"You are missin' me."

"Every time I throw somethin' in your direction. How's Dufus doin'?"

"Only thing he's moved since you left is his right elbow. He doesn't seem to know what to do with hisself. Julep has eaten narly a thing. Runaway just stands against the fence starin' at the house."

"You're makin' me feel better, Tandy. You truly are."

"How was that big party your uncle and aunt threw for you last night?"

"It wasn't exactly for me. I was sort of let in. They dressed me up as some kind of a clown."

"So you acted the clown."

"You got it."

"Your cousins up there got any interestin' friends?"

"Well, they must be interestin' to theirselves. They don't seem to extend themselves to others much, if you dig what I say."

"You played the trumpet for them?"

"I did."

"I'll bet that got 'em goin'."

"Oh, yeah. I got 'em goin' all right. Got 'em goin' home."

"You met any girl yet you like better'n me?"

"I met one I like a lot."

"What's her name?"

"Ginny. Virginia. We took a canoe trip together yesterday on the river. Had a picnic."

"What's she look like?"

"Pretty cute in a bikini."

"Hussy. Bet she don't make you laugh like I do."

"She's pretty funny."

"Skylar! I hope your nose falls into your lap, I do! I knew you'd be this way! Gone from home four, five days and some girl already has you yanked sideways. You're supposed to miss me a little bit. It's only natural!"

"You're the one who tol' me I had to come up here."

"You fixin' to marry up with this Gin person?"

"What Gin person?"

"That girl you were just carryin' on about."

"You mean my thirteen-year-old cousin, Ginny? What do you think I am, a European royal?"

"Oh, Skylar!"

"How are you and Jimmy Bob doin'?"

There was a moment of silence on the line. "Well, my teeth were sore there for a while. But they tightened up again okay."

"What're you talkin' about, your teeth?"

"Oh. Your question made me think someone had tol' you. Your mother or someone. Well, Jimmy Bob slapped me—well, he punched me, real hard, on my mouth."

"He did what?"

"I saw stars, like that time I fell off that horse and landed my head on the brick wall? Blood dribbled down my chin onto that nice white shirt you gave me? I thought some of my teeth were goin' to come out. They wiggled around like suckling pigs under a sow's belly."

"Tandy, what are you talkin' about? Jimmy Bob hit you?"

"Well, maybe I deserved it."

"NEVER! Never say that. Never think it."

"Our wedding's less than two weeks away, Skylar. He wants us to, you know, start actin' like man and wife now. He says he wouldn't buy a pickup truck without drivin' it first."

"You're not a pickup! Is he that stupid he thinks that's what marriage is? He thinks it's about drivin' you like a truck?"

"I haven't been puttin' out for him, Skylar." Her voice dropped. "Can't stand the thought of it. After you."

"What are you sayin'? Then why are you fixin' to marry up with him?"

"He drives an eighteen-wheeler, Skylar. Long-haul. You'll never drive an eighteen-wheeler, now will you? You'll never settle down, leastways not here in Greendowns County, any more'n Runaway will comb his own mane. You've already played your trumpet both in the Holler and the Baptist church. There's not much else for you here, is there? I'll be a good wife to Jimmy Bob, eventually. We'll have kids."

"Tandy, I thought you had some likin' for him. You tol' me he reads books—"

"That was some drivin' manual."

"He makes jokes—"

"About people."

"Tandy—"

"He's dreadful jealous of you, Skylar. He knows you and I have been screwin' around together since we were children. Since Mama first put us in the bathtub together, we've never stopped. That makes Jimmy Bob dreadful mad."

"Tandy, don't you marry Jimmy Bob. You hear me?"

"I can't keep livin' on your parents' farm the rest of my natural days, Skylar."

"You do plenty of work. More'n anybody."

"I got to get my own life goin'."

"Where's Dufus?"

"Now don't you do anything, Skylar. You'll just make things worse. It'll be all right. Jimmy Bob's drivin' a load of dashboards to Michigan tomorrow or the next day, and then somethin' else on to California. By the time he gets back it will be just another week afore we get married, and I expect he'll have someplace to go that week, so maybe all that time on the road by hisself will give him time to cogitate, maybe cool hisself down."

"Tandy, I hate this."

"I didn't mean to tell you all this. I really didn't. My teeth are fine. You've got to get your education, Skylar. I tol' you that. Make us all proud. And I'll make you proud, too. Produce a bunch of square, hairy kids with flat noses. Guess we've talked enough. Too much. 'Bye, Skylar."

The phone went dead.

Coming slowly up the block in the patrol car, Bernard asked Clarence, "What's that noise?"

"Someone's playin' a trumpet." Clarence cocked his ear toward the car's open window. "Damn well, too. Must be some kind of a stereo."

"Look. It's that damned boy, sittin' on the stoop. I told you so, Clarence."

"You told me what?"

"He's trouble. Makin' that terrible noise."

"It's a beautiful noise he's makin', Bernard. Just listen to him."

"Pull up. I want to speak to him." Through the window of the patrol car, Bernard glared at Skylar until he stopped playing. Bernard said, "Boy! Get yourself over here!"

Skylar did not move. "Who you callin' 'boy'?" he drawled.

"You, you young imbecile!" Bernard snarled. "Get your damned near-bare ass over here before I come after you with my truncheon!"

Skylar sauntered over to the patrol car. "I only came over," Skylar said, "to find out what the heck a truncheon is. Whatever you said."

"You live here, in that house?"

Skylar surveyed the rooming house. "You could say that. Considerin' what you Yankees appear to think is 'livin.' "

"Oh, my God, Clarence. A Southern boy. His talkin' is a worse racket than his horn playin'!" He asked Skylar, "How long have you graced our fair city, lad?"

"What?"

"How long you been in town?"

"Two, three hours. Haven't enjoyed a minute of it, either."

"You own a shirt?"

"Yes, sir. Two or three."

"Why aren't you wearin' one?"

"Hot. Shirt I had on earlier got soakin' wet." Skylar looked at the wetness of the police officers' shirts under their armpits. He wrinkled his nose.

"Why are you playin' that horn in a public street?"

"Tryin' to drown out the screekin'."

"What screechin'? Are you stoned, boy? What screechin' are you hearin'?"

"That screekin'!" Skylar pointed to the roofs along

the street. "The screekin' those damned ventilators are makin'!"

"Do you hear a screechin', Clarence?"

"You don't even hear it!" Skylar said. "How can you not hear it? How can you stand it?"

"You know, Bernard," Clarence said, "we don't hear the screechin' anymore."

"What screechin'? Are you both balmy? And I don't want to hear your horn anymore!" Bernard said.

"Why not?" Skylar asked.

"You're disturbin' the peace."

Skylar raised his eyebrows. "You found peace? God loves ya!"

"You put that horn away!" Bernard shouted. "Don't you ever play it again! Ever!"

Clarence moved the car forward.

"Where are you goin'?" Bernard asked him. "I wasn't done with him!"

"Yes, you were." Clarence turned the corner slowly. "You told that young man not ever to play his trumpet again."

"I did. Yes."

"Ever?" Clarence asked. "Did you mean 'ever'?"

"I did, yes. I do."

Pointing at the roofs, Skylar yelled at the slow-moving police car. "It's those damned ventilators disturbin' the peace! Not Candoli!"

"What's he shoutin', Clarence?"

"I think he called you a gamboli, Bernard."

"What's a gamboli?"

"I think it's Southern talk, Bernard, for an old pig with hair in his ears."

* * *

Still sitting on the stoop, Skylar kept his trumpet in his lap.

Dusk was falling.

A heavy, balding man crossed the road. He stopped in front of Skylar.

The man smiled. "Hi."

"Ha," Skylar said.

"Let me hear you play your trumpet," the man said.

"Can't."

"Why not?"

"The police officers told me not to."

"I don't see any police officers around here."

"They come screekin' out of the ventilators."

"Where are you from?" the man asked.

"Heaven," Skylar answered.

"Is that the name of some Southern town?"

"All of 'em."

"What are you doing in Boston?"

"I came all the way up here to be told to shut my face. Leastwise, I haven't learned much else so far."

"You want a hundred dollars?"

"Sure."

"What are you willing to do for it? And how long?"

"Heavy lifting. You want something moved?" Skylar looked around, trying to figure from where the man had come.

The man giggled.

"Light carpentry, I can do. Paintin'?"

"You turn me on." The man looked up at the house. "You have a room here?"

"I can castrate a bull calf," Skylar said. "You like to eat mountain oysters?"

"I don't know. I've never had any," the man said. "I'll try anything you say."

"How about goin' away?"

The man put his hand on Skylar's leg. "Now why would I do that?"

" 'Cause here come the cops?"

"Clarence! Now look at the young son of a bitch! Just as I thought! Sellin' himself in the public street! Didn't I just tell you?"

The man talking to Skylar saw the approaching patrol car. And fled rapidly along the sidewalk.

"I don't believe it," Clarence said. "Better he should play the trumpet."

"And the bald-faced boy doesn't even have the decency to disappear into the house! Look at the way he just sits there! Glarin' at us, he is!"

"Glarin' at you, Bernard. You're the one made him give up the trumpet."

"Stop the car! Let me out!" Bernard slid his baton into its holster.

"Now, Bernard . . ."

"Stop the car! And no more of your nonsense."

Clarence followed Bernard across the sidewalk.

"You know what solicitation is, boy?" Bernard shouted at Skylar.

"Is that anything like yelling in a public road?" Skylar asked quietly.

"What's your name, boy?"

Aloud, Skylar read the police officer's name tag. "Bernard Leary," he said. "Good name for you. Be leery."

"Up close, you know, Clarence, I seem to recognize this boy from somewhere. Do you?"

"No."

"I've seen a picture of him somewhere. Very recently. Are you wanted, son?"

"Clearly," said Clarence.

"What were you talkin' to that man about?"

"Mountain oysters," Skylar said.

"What's that, when they're at home?"

"Balls," Skylar said. "Bulls' balls."

Bernard fingered his baton. "Don't you swear at me, you little turd."

"In fact, Bernard, we do not have this young man on a prostitution charge."

"Prostitution? Skylar?"

A young woman joined them from the sidewalk. She carried a flight bag.

"Ha, Terri," Skylar said.

"The fuzz have you on a prostitution charge, Skylar?" Terri Ainsley laughed. "What were you soliciting—brass, reeds, and percussion?"

"These police officers came along and told me to stop playin' my horn, Terri. Then this other man came along and asked me to play my horn." Skylar looked up at the ventilators on the roofs. "I knew that screekin' must drive people crazy. 'Course, you all been here longer'n I have."

"You know this young man?" Clarence asked Terri.

"Oh, yes." Terri smiled. "This boy raises a fuss everywhere he goes. But he's not a bad boy; just a little slow. Please, Officers, if you place him in my custody, I'll do my best to keep him off the streets."

Terri Ainsley and Skylar Whitfield went up the steps to the house together.

"Well!" Bernard's face was red. "I'm glad that girl is no daughter of mine!"

"Sure." Clarence laughed. "You'll have your

daughters home forever, washin' your stinky shirts, you will. . . ."

"What's in the bag?" Skylar asked.

They were climbing the three flights of stairs to his room.

"My hair dryer. My toothbrush. A change of clothes. A submarine sandwich. A bottle of Pepsi-Cola. Papers I'll need for me to register at Knightsbridge tomorrow."

"Planning on camping out tonight?"

"Some condoms. I was thinking of it. If I can find a good campsite." She stepped into Skylar's fourth-floor room. "Hot. No air conditioner?"

"Windows. That damnable screekin' . . ."

"This used to be a servant's room. A maid's room."

"Did maids always use to have to wear shirts? Poor them."

"Oh, Skylar." Terri put her hand flat against his chest. She kissed his chin. "Where's the bathroom?"

"Down the hall, Mrs. Fitz said."

In the bathroom they found a huge, long, deep, claw-footed Victorian bathtub.

Terri closed the door. She adjusted the faucets on the tub. "Lukewarm," she said. "We want it lukewarm."

"We do? You plannin' to breed newts in there?"

"Is this all right?" She undid the only button on his shorts. Then she cupped her hand over his crotch. Her eyes shone into his. "Did I call you 'a little slow'?"

"I'll try to be."

She was not wearing a bra under her shirt.

"Hoo, boy," Skylar said.

"Beg pardon?"

"Hoo, girl."

"You were supposed to ask me something."

"What?"

"If it was all right for you to take off my shirt."

"Was it?" He was working on her shorts.

"Sure. But you haven't asked if it's all right to take off my shorts."

"Is it?" Her shorts dropped to the floor.

"I'm not sure. It depends on what you want to do."

"Take off your socks. Your sneakers." Gently he guided her so that she was sitting on the edge of the tall tub. "Your pants."

"Then what?"

Kneeling, he was baring her feet.

"You're supposed to ask, Skylar."

"Okay, I'll ask: Where are the newts? In your flight bag?"

"Don't you get it?"

He sat back on his heels and looked at her. "Get what? 'Cept you're talkin' an awful lot."

"We're supposed to permit each other."

" 'Permit each other'? What does that mean?"

"Talk to each other. Make sure everything we do is all right with the other."

"Aren't our bodies talkin' to each other? Aren't we givin' each other permission for what we're doin' by the way we're respondin'?"

"The tub's full." Terri stood up, turned around, and turned off the taps. "Will you sit at the tap end?"

"Will you get onto the bed first?" In his room, Terri had turned back the spread and blanket.

"Why?"

"You'd be less frightening that way."

Through the two small windows, Skylar saw it was dark outside. To him, the sky glowed eerily with city light.

" 'Frightening'? I frighten you?" Together they had played, and talked, in the tub more than forty minutes.

"I know." Hands folded behind his head, she kissed his cheek. "So far, you've been very gentle."

"If I frighten you, why are you here?"

"I didn't expect you to be so gentle."

He kept his hands at his sides. Was he supposed to ask her if he could put his arms around her and bring her to him, press their naked bodies together? Kiss her? He guessed not. She had already implied not. He was to get on the bed.

He sat on the edge of the bed.

"I don't know," he said. "Why did you come here?"

She knelt on the bed. "To make love with you."

"Why would you want to make love with me if you don't trust me?"

"Have you a condom?"

"Playing," he said, "lovemaking, is a natural thing. A carnal thing. Do you know the word *carnal*? Or is that just a Baptist word?"

Her cupped hand waggled his penis. "Right now, buddy, all the blood from your brain is down here."

"If it's to be any good, our bodies have got to be free to respond to each other, naturally, carnally. If one of us does something that hurts the other, or the other doesn't like, our bodies will know it, react, tell the other, go in a different direction. Don't you trust your own body, Terri?"

"We can agree with each other first," Terri said. "I mean, verbally."

"How about spontaneity?"

"That can go too far. I mean, who's to be in control of the spontaneity? You?"

"Good grief. You. Me. We! Spontaneity is what happens when we're in control together! Making love, you know? Moving, acting together!"

"Okay, but let's talk about it first."

"If you want to talk about sex, why don't you go to a pajama party?"

"Why are you being so unpleasant? Are you that much of an unreconstructed male?"

"What?"

She stretched out on the bed. "For a while, just hug me and kiss me. But no finger stuff. You know what I mean? Not yet."

He stretched out alongside her.

"Wrap your legs around me," she said. "No. Leave my ear alone."

His legs around her waist, he flattened his back against the bed. He sighed. "This isn't lovemaking," he said. "This is negotiating."

"What's wrong with you?" she asked.

"This way," Skylar said, "you and I are goin' nowhere, girl."

"I'll tell you when to put the condom on," she said. "I have some in my flight bag."

"Lordy, Lordy," Skylar said. "This is what it must be like having your mother watching us."

"Which side of the bed do you want to sleep on?" Terri asked.

"The middle."

"I prefer the left."

During that evening, Terri and Skylar had negotiated their way through copulation twice.

Between times, sitting naked, cross-legged on the bed, silently they had eaten their submarine sandwiches and drunk their Pepsi-Cola.

After he turned out the light, they lay on the bed, naked, not touching. It was too hot to draw a sheet over them.

Ventilators were screeching. Terri had not mentioned being bothered by the noise, or even being aware of it. The two little windows under the eaves had to be open for whatever air was flowing.

Lordy, Lordy, Skylar said to himself. I am not long for this world.

In the dark, she said, "Skylar?"

"Yes?"

"I was hoping you'd give me an orgasm."

He asked, "Have you ever had an orgasm?"

"No."

No, Skylar said to himself: I am not long for this world.

Chapter 18

"Whitfield, Skylar?" someone shouted.

"Yo!!" Skylar raised his hand over the other heads in the hall.

Labor Day morning he was standing in line with Terri Ainsley outside the registrar's office at Knightsbridge School of Music.

A young man approached him and said, "Report to Room One-twelve, Professor Pintree, Skylar, before you register. You haven't auditioned yet."

"I have to audition? I've got a scholarship."

"He's trumpet," Terri said. "Pintree. Big genius. You haven't played for him yet?"

"Tapes," Skylar said. "He's heard some tapes. Or somebody has. That's how I got the scholarship."

"Probably just wants to talk to you," Terri said. "You'll be in his department mostly."

Skylar looked at the place he would be losing in the long line. "Boy, oh, boy." He picked up his trumpet case off the floor. In a manila envelope in his other hand he had all the papers he believed he needed to register. "People say Southerners talk a lot." He followed the directions to Room 112 the young man had given him. "Nothin' beats a Yankee with nothin' to say."

"You Whitfield?" The man waiting in Room 112 was as skinny as six o'clock. He was perhaps forty years old. To Skylar, the man's eyes looked like two dead beetles on snow. "Or a half-wit field?"

"Sir?"

"Close the door. Play 'Flight of the Bumblebee.'"

Taking his trumpet out of his case, in a low voice Skylar asked, "Are you serious?"

"Of course I'm serious. Why do you even question me?"

"Just thought," Skylar said. "Chestnut . . ."

"Play it."

As Skylar played the first bars, Pintree turned to the window. "Yes!" he said.

Then he turned around and watched Skylar. He came closer to Skylar. His dead eyes squinted as he watched Skylar play. "No!" he shouted. "Stop!"

Skylar stopped.

"You know nothing about proper fingering." Skylar said nothing. "Great tone. Great speed. Dexterity. You sound good. No wonder you were able to fool everybody with an audiotape. But you've never learned to play the trumpet, have you?"

"I've had to muddle along by myself," Skylar admitted.

"Never had a lesson in your life?"

"Not really. I learned to read music by myself. Well, Mrs. Abelard, the church organist? She gave me the first clue as to how to do that."

"Nothing we can do with you," Pintree said.

"Sir?"

"Whitfield, you'd be better off if you'd never seen a trumpet before. We could teach you proper fingering. You've got so many bad habits, I doubt now you could ever learn proper fingering. Not if you live to be a hundred."

"It works," Skylar said. "You said I have tone, speed, dexterity."

"You don't know how to play the trumpet. It's that simple. No orchestra would ever have you. Not even a first-class jazz band."

"I don't care about no orchestra."

"You'd never be able to teach."

"I don't plan to. I came here to learn music. How to write it. Composition. Orchestration."

"Okay. Play me something you've written." Pintree turned his back on him. "I can't stand to watch you."

Skylar began to play "Maxiflirt in a Miniskirt."

"Stop." Pintree, face lowered, turned around again. "That's pretty."

"Thanks."

"I mean, that's pretty. Melodic."

"Thanks."

Dead eyes fixed on Skylar. "Idiot! That's not a compliment! You know nothing about music! You're playing music that is linear!"

"I am?"

"Where did you . . . what music have you heard in your life? Let me guess. Church music!"

"Yes, sir."

"The junk out of your Baptist church, I'll bet! Hymns! The stupid stuff out of Nashville!"

"I hardly ever been there, sir."

"A few classics thrown in! All that stuff is linear!"

"What does that mean?"

"Whitfield, the young people who come to Knightsbridge come here already knowing a whole lot more about music than you do. They put the stuff you're playing behind them by the time they were thirteen years old, if they ever heard it or paid it any attention at all. Your musical sense hasn't even formed, your sense of modern music. Your mind isn't even ready for it. Probably never will be. Trying to teach you modern music would be like trying to teach Cicero modern American English." Pintree shook a wide open hand at him. "Your music is pretty!"

"I'm sorry, sir." More embarrassed than ever he had been in his life, Skylar stood holding his trumpet in front of him. He wondered if this is how most people feel when first seen naked and lacking. He asked, "What do we do about it?"

"Go home to Nashville."

"I'm not from Nashville."

"I can do nothing for you. Life isn't that long."

On one knee, Skylar was putting his trumpet back in his case.

"Dean Winters wants to see you."

"Who's Dean Winters?"

"His office is next to the registrar's."

Pintree had opened the door. He stood mocking patience while Skylar left the room.

Pintree added nothing to what he had said.

After sitting on a bench for twenty minutes, Skylar was shown into a small office. Scores were on wide bookshelves. On the walls over the bookshelves were framed prints of musical instruments.

Dean Winters remained seated behind his desk.

On his desk was a newspaper.

Winters glanced at Skylar. "I thought so. How many Skylar Whitfields can there be?"

"Only one, I guess, that I know of."

"Whitfield . . ." The dean spoke slowly. "You any idea what it means to file a false financial report?"

"Sir?"

"I have here"—the dean picked up some papers from a folder—"your application for a scholarship to Knightsbridge School of Music. Which scholarship was granted you, with certain contingencies."

"No one ever wrote me about any certain contingencies."

"There are always contingencies." He handed Skylar a piece of paper. "Is that a true accounting of the financial condition of your family?"

Skylar did not need to look at the paper. He had filled it out himself.

"Yes, sir."

"Your father's income? Your mother's income? Their assets?"

"Yes, sir. Roughly. As well as I knew."

" 'Roughly.' " The dean turned the newspaper around on his desk, so Skylar could read it. "Are these pictures in yesterday's Style section of you?"

Skylar leaned to look at the newspaper. "Oh, Lord."

"Real cute," the dean said. " 'Creation of David Lowenstein.' Are you a creation of David Lowenstein?"

There were two pictures of Skylar on the page. The first was of him and Jon dressed in Mr. Lowenstein's 'summer tuxedos' coming down the beautiful stairs to the foyer of Paxton Landing, with the formally dressed, very pretty Jonesy and Terri accompanying them.

The second was of Terri on one foot, her other foot raised behind her, kissing Skylar.

"Poor boy from Tennessee, huh?" the dean asked.

"Sir . . ."

"Your family is one of the richest in the country. Your uncle is CEO of Calder Partners. Your aunt is a Calder, if I'm not mistaken. And you want us to deprive some other young person of money he or she really needs to attend Knightsbridge so you can come here and cut a swath through high society? I don't think so. . . ."

Skylar exhaled as if he had been punched in the stomach.

"Now, listen, Skylar Whitfield . . . if your family wants the prestige of your having a scholarship to attend Knightsbridge School of Music, maybe we'll understand. It depends on what your family will do for us."

"What? I don't . . ."

"Donations are always acceptable. We need a new wing to our main building. A new auditorium. The acoustics in the old hall are atrocious. Maybe your family could see their way to committing to a schedule of donations to the Knightsbridge School of Music? . . . Yes, Ms. Fayle?"

A woman had entered the office. She stood well behind, away from Skylar. She seemed short of breath.

"Police are here. Warrant for the arrest of Skylar Whitfield. Rape."

"WHAT?" The sound exploded from Skylar.

The dean looked interested.

The next minutes were a blur for Skylar.

Two men entered the office. One wore a uniform, the other a suit. While the man in the suit recited Skylar his rights, the uniformed policeman strapped Skylar's hands behind his back with a strip of plastic.

"My trumpet," Skylar said.

"I'll bring it," the man in the suit said. "What about this envelope?"

"You can leave that," Skylar said. "Guess I won't be needing it."

Holding Skylar's left bicep, the uniformed policeman led Skylar on wobbling knees out of the office and down the corridor. The people they passed drew back and stared.

Terri Ainsley was in the front hall of the building. She held her flight bag.

"Terri!" Skylar said. "How could you do me this way?"

As he was being led through the front door, he called back to her, "I'm sorry you didn't achieve orgasm, girl! I swear it wasn't all my fault!"

Chapter 19

Alex Broadbent stood at the edge of the swimming pool at Paxton Landing watching Joan Appleyard swim laps. Turning at one end, she glanced up at him.

At the shallow end she stopped and stood up.

"You want to talk to me, Mr. Broadbent?"

"If you don't mind."

In her string bikini Jonesy walked out of and around the pool.

Alex thought her an uncommonly good-looking young woman.

He sat on a chair under an umbrella. He lit a cigarette.

Wet, towel in hand, she, too, sat.

"Where's Jon?" Alex asked.

"I haven't seen him since sometime yesterday. Or was it the night before? I have no idea where he is." Tossing her hair with the towel, she said, "I've hardly seen anyone. The old place is very quiet. People with briefcases are coming and going. Meetings seem to be going on continuously in Mr. Whitfield's study. I'm really just waiting to make my manners to Mr. and Mrs. Whitfield before going home."

"Um," Alex uttered. "Jonesy, Skylar just called me. From a Boston jail." She said nothing. "He has been arrested and questioned. Apparently, late yesterday you went to the local police here in Paxton and charged Skylar with two counts of rape." For some reason, Jonesy looked surprised. "I've asked the Boston police to keep him there, not to transfer him to the police out here in Paxton until you and I straighten this out."

Jonesy continued to look somewhat surprised, even perplexed. Still she said nothing.

Alex said, "You have charged that Skylar entered your bedroom while you were asleep and raped you about dawn Saturday morning, and a second time, after the party, again in your bedroom, again after you were asleep, Saturday night. Is that right?"

Her eyes flashed at Alex. "You think you and I can 'straighten this out'?"

"There seems to be some confusion here I would like to help clarify."

"I don't see that this is any of your business, Mr. Broadbent."

"I think you'll discover it is my business, and why Skylar called me. Otherwise, you are right: I wouldn't interfere."

"Isn't this called men sticking together in the face of a woman's injury? Isn't this called intimidation?"

"No, Jonesy. You know better than that from reading me."

Jonesy sighed. Her glance at Alex was uncertain, possibly fearful. Then she said, "Yes. I do."

"Okay."

"What confusion?"

"Well, for example, you just said you are waiting to 'make your manners,' say good-bye to Lacey and Wayne Whitfield, whose nephew you have just charged with rape, in their home? Have you told them you have brought these most serious charges against Skylar?"

"No. Dr. MacBride told Mrs Whitfield about... what happened, what happened the first time, Saturday afternoon. Apparently, she didn't take the report seriously. She did nothing about it."

"Nevertheless, you're waiting to thank her for her hospitality? What sense does that make?"

Jonesy studied the tops of the trees.

"If Skylar raped you early Saturday morning, and his aunt, your hostess, was so informed by a professional counselor, and Lacey did nothing about it, why did you even stay in the house Saturday night?"

"I don't know. I don't think I quite believed it myself."

Alex said, "To some extent your story has been corroborated by your psychiatrist, a Dr. MacBride, in that you reported this 'event' to her Saturday morning, and talked to her again Sunday."

"I have that right."

"Of course you do. She telephoned the Paxton police herself last evening."

"She said she would."

"Seeing a doctor has been involved, a psychiatrist who is also necessarily a medical doctor, have you been medically examined? Is there any physical evidence these rapes took place?"

"No."

"Why not?"

"She wanted to get away for the weekend. I had already delayed her enough."

"She could have had another doctor examine you."

"She suggested it."

"And you refused?"

"Yes."

"Why?"

"I don't know."

"Haven't you already answered that question?"

"What do you mean?"

"That you didn't 'quite believe it yourself'? That the rape happened?"

"I don't know."

"The only reason Skylar can think why you brought these charges against him is because, he says, you 'hit on him,' propositioned him most explicitly both Friday evening and Saturday evening. And because both times he rejected you. He rejected you because you are his cousin's fiancée. Is any of that true?"

"Maybe. I don't know. We'd been partying both nights. There's something wrong with Skylar."

"What?"

"He bothers me."

"Sure."

"Dr. MacBride is my psychiatrist, Mr. Broadbent. Not you. Aren't you practicing psychiatry without a license?"

"No. Tell me, Jonesy, which of the two nights are you the more certain Skylar raped you?"

"Saturday night. After the party."

"Why?"

"Because it exhausted me. All yesterday, I was bone-weary. Every muscle in my body ached. I was shaky, shivering. So hungry. So thirsty. Yet sort of nauseous. I couldn't think about anything else. I still can't."

"So you are certain Skylar raped you Saturday night?"

"Yes."

"And that's what you will say when you testify against him?"

Jonesy said nothing.

"Jonesy? Are you listening?"

"Yes."

"Except for ten or twelve minutes all Saturday night, Skylar was not out of my sight."

She stared at Alex with big eyes. "You say."

"We all say. Everyone who was staying at my house. After the party, Skylar came home with me. We all talked, listened to music, looked at some abstract videos. . . . Still listening?"

"Yes."

"During those ten or twelve minutes he was out of my sight, Skylar was rescuing his cousin Calder and Tom Palmer from drowning. Driving drunk on the old timber road, Tom hit a tree at high speed and flipped the car over, upside down into the river. They were trapped and unconscious under the car. How on earth Skylar dragged them out and revived them is a wonder."

"Is that true? I've heard nothing about it."

"Absolutely true. Again, many witnesses. Myself. My houseguests. Wayne Whitfield. Obadiah. The chauffeur . . ."

Between the two sitting under an umbrella next to the swimming pool, there was a long silence.

The pool water had evaporated completely from Jonesy's skin.

Tears began to run down her cheeks.

She stammered, "It was a dream, dreaming? It didn't happen? They did not happen?"

Alex did not answer.

Jonesy said, "I told Dr. MacBride I wasn't sure . . . that I could have dreamed it."

"She told you to go to the police? File the charges against Skylar?"

"Yes. She said, for my own emotional health. Something had happened. Skylar had done something to me. Harmed me. Upset me."

"I guess he did. But he didn't rape you."

"No. I guess he didn't. He did not."

"And it was you who went to the police, you who filed charges."

"Yes."

"I'm afraid it's for you to clean up this mess."

"Yes." She looked at the towel in her lap. "Say it to me simply."

"It's okay. Dreams can be very real. Sometimes they can seem more real than reality. We all know that. These dreams . . . I guess maybe you wanted them to be real."

"I did. But why would I want to harm Skylar? Do this to him?"

"Truly, I'm not playing psychiatrist."

"It seemed so real. My bed was a mess, like it never has been. I believed something must have happened, been real. The sheets smelled of . . ."

"Jonesy, I don't think you were lying on purpose."

"But, why . . . how could I do such a thing? So convince myself? Are you sure?"

"I can't account for Skylar's whereabouts Friday night, except that he had just spent forty hours or so on a bus. But Saturday night, besides being with me, us, he was busy saving the lives of two people. And when he was done with that, he was the one who was as weak and shaken as a newborn kitten. That I guarantee you."

"I'm sorry. So sorry. Do you think it could be the prescription pills I've been taking . . . that made me do this thing . . . that made it all seem so real?"

"Come on. Get dressed. Get your luggage. I'll go with you. First you need to go to the Paxton police station and take back your statements. Then let's go into Boston together and get Skylar out of the clink."

"You'll come with me?"

"I'll drive you. I think I should. Don't you?"

"Jon . . ." Jonesy looked toward the house. "The Whitfields . . . Whatever will they think?"

"That there's been some confusion. And that you were ill-advised."

"I never smelled anyone like Skylar before."

Alex grinned. "I'm not about to ask you how Skylar smells."

"At dinner Friday night . . . He is so happy about just being a male. I'd never met anyone like him. His cracked English . . . but somehow he knows, way deep inside him, he is perfectly all right. I saw this when he was playing in the swimming pool with Ginny and Jon Friday afternoon." Forearms over her breasts, she put her hands on her own shoulders. "I wanted him all over me. Do you understand that? I wanted him to be him, with me, on me, in me. . . ."

"Never mind about that now." Alex stood up. "While you're getting ready to go, I think I should call your Dr. MacBride. Don't you?"

"Please. She ought to be back from her weekend by now. Explain all this to her, how terribly wrong I was. Yes. I must apologize to Skylar. I'm so sorry. Have I made a lot of trouble?"

Towel in hand, Jonesy stopped on the steps to the

upper terrace. "Tell me, Mr. Broadbent, can Skylar sue me now? Can he sue Dr. MacBride? For false arrest or something?"

Alex said, "I'm not practicing law, either. Let's go."

Chapter 20

Coming through the door of that Boston police station, Alex said to Skylar, "I've got my car. Why don't I give you a ride back to wherever you're staying?"

"Thank you." Skylar got into the front passenger seat of Alex Broadbent's Volvo wagon. " 'Specially since I have no idea where I am. Or why."

"I'm sorry, so sorry," Jonesy had said to Skylar in the lobby of the police station. "I don't know what got into me."

"I didn't." Carrying his trumpet, Skylar headed straight for the front door of the police station. "That's for damned sure!"

On the steps entering the police station, Officer Bernard Leary had smiled broadly when he saw Skylar. "Goddamn it, boy! I knew I'd see you here! What're you charged with?"

"Assaulting a police officer," Skylar answered. "Be leery."

Alex drove the Volvo away from the curb.

On the sidewalk stood Joan Appleyard and Dr.

MacBride. Both frowning women silently stared at Alex Broadbent and Skylar Whitfield in the car as it drove away.

Skylar told Alex the address of his rooming house. "I'd also sure appreciate it, Mr. Broadbent, if you then carried me to the bus station? It won't take me a minute to pack."

"Where are you going?"

"Home."

"What about Knightsbridge?"

"It didn't work out."

"Why?"

"My fingering works okay, the man said, but I guess it just didn't look right to him. He said my music is too pretty. I was given the impression people might could actually hum along to it."

Alex said, "Oh, no! We'd hate to have the populace humming, even singing again!"

"Also, that there dean saw those pictures of me in the newspaper yesterday, lookin' like a circus pony."

"So did I. Circus pony is about right. Too bad there weren't pictures of you looking more like a porpoise pulling people from the river a few hours later."

"Uncle Wayne has told me to shut up about that."

"Of course."

"So the dean said I filed a fraudulent financial statement to get the scholarship. He said, if I'm to enjoy the prestige of a scholarship to Knightsbridge, I need to hit up my uncle Wayne and aunt Lacey for a new wing to their building or something. I don't quite get the arithmetic of that, do you?"

"Well, Knightsbridge . . ."

"Knightsbridge what?"

"Knightsbridge is not the most prestigious music school in the country, Skylar. Not even in Boston."

"Then, while I was in the dean's office, I was arrested for rape. I didn't notice anybody rushin' to my defense, tryin' to protect me, offerin' to make any phone calls for me. It was hours before I could call you."

Alex exhaled cigarette smoke. "Clearly, Jonesy was ill-advised. And she said something about some prescription pills she's been taking." Alex watched Skylar's face.

"I don't care. I'm goin' home. All I know is that since I've been here in Yankeeland, all I've been told is to shut up, shut my face, hush my mouth, and don't be me. Well, sir, I can't think of anybody I'd rather be."

"Good for you. But your music—"

" 'The more music lessons,' " Skylar recited, " 'the more music lessens.' "

Alex chuckled. "But . . ."

"I sure appreciate what you've done for me, are doin' for me, Mr. Broadbent. When I first met you Saturday night and you told me I might need you, I had no idea what you were talkin' about."

"Neither did I. Exactly." Alex turned left and then right into an alley to avoid red lights on the cross streets. "Skylar, I'd like you to come back to Paxton Landing before you go home."

"Why?"

"Something's wrong there."

"What? Calder nearly drowned. She's recoverin', isn't she?"

"Something else. I don't know what. I just feel something is wrong. It's Labor Day. The place is as quiet as a mausoleum. Jonesy told me she hasn't seen Jonathan since Saturday night; people with briefcases are coming and going quietly. Meetings of some sort are going on continuously. Usually Ginny and Louise are in and out, up and down. I haven't noticed either of them since I guess sometime Saturday."

"Ha!" Skylar said. "Jon, Ginny, and Louise Uglythorpe heisted those gembobs and headed for the border!"

"I rather doubt that. I tried calling. Obadiah said he knows nothing, of course; he was just told to stop all calls."

"There's a parking space."

"One thing I can tell you," Alex said. "I made a few quiet phone calls. Those gembobs weren't insured."

"Not?"

"Your uncle Wayne stopped paying the premiums in July."

"Wow. Why would he do that?"

"Carelessness? He forgot? He was in the hospital in July. But I expect he has people paying his routine bills automatically."

"Then why?"

"Could he be broke?"

"Uncle Wayne broke? The Calders—"

"Such things happen. The mighty do fall. It takes awhile for it to catch up to them. But they do fall. Silently, at first."

"Well, sir, if that's the case, I can see how things just might have quieted down around the old place. Do you suppose those folks know how not to be rich?"

In Skylar's room, Jon sat slumped in the Morris chair.

"What are you doing here?" Skylar asked. "Not

that you're not as welcome as anyone who looks worse'n I do."

"Mrs. Fitz let me in. She said she loved your trumpet playing yesterday afternoon, Skylar." Wanly, Jon grinned. "She also told me you have a friend. Who spent the night with you."

"Not a friend I expect to bring home to Mama." Skylar got his suitcase from the bottom of the wardrobe.

Alex sat on the bed. "I do believe, Jonathan, this is the first time I've ever seen you unshaven."

"I've been driving, driving, driving," Jon said. "All night. All day. Cruising the roads. Driving back and forth, Logan Airport, the bus station, the train stations."

"Why?" Alex asked.

"Looking for a thirteen-year-old girl in a pink party dress. Where could she be? I suppose by now she could have begged, borrowed, bought other clothes . . . but still . . ."

Alex and Skylar looked at each other, and then, both, at Jon.

Alex asked, "Are you talking about Ginny?"

"Dad told me to shut up."

"Of course," Alex said.

"Damn right," said Skylar.

Jon took a deep breath. "Sunday morning, walking Rufus, Dot Palmer saw Ginny on the Oglethorps' lawn. In Ginny's hand was a pistol, probably that pistol Mother kept in her bedside table. When Ginny saw Dot, she dropped the pistol and ran away. She hasn't been seen or heard from since."

"Big deal." Skylar opened the suitcase. "Ginny got caught playing with a gun. Where I come from—"

"Louise Oglethorp was under a nearby tree, shot through the head."

Slowly, Skylar sat on the bed beside Alex.

Slowly, Alex got up and went to stare through the open window.

In the silence, Skylar heard the screeching of the roof ventilators.

Head in hands, Jon said, "I can't find her!"

From the window, Alex's voice rasped. He still sounded as might an Old Testament prophet. "Louise . . . Can't envision . . . Ginny?" He cleared his throat. "I don't know where to start."

"Finding Ginny," Jon said. "Trying to find Ginny."

Alex turned and looked at Skylar. "I don't know how. How does a child hide? In the house? In some linen closet? Wouldn't she be afraid to run too far, where she wouldn't feel safe?"

Red-eyed, Jon looked at Alex. "I didn't expect to find you here, Mr. Broadbent. I mean, with Skylar. Why are you here? Did you know anything about all this?"

"No," Alex said. "I wish I still didn't. Someone needed to get Skylar out of jail."

"Skylar? In jail?"

"Someone charged Skylar with two counts of rape," Alex said. "We needn't bother with that right this instant."

Jon's face wrinkled. "Who? Who charged Skylar with rape?"

"Your fiancée," Alex said. "Joan Appleyard."

Jon said, "It never happened."

"No," Alex said. "We were able to prove that. Her fantasies may have been at least partly caused by some pills her psychiatrist was giving her."

"Yes," Jon said. "That and more. Have the charges been dropped?"

"Dropped and expunged from the record," Alex said. "All a terrible mistake."

"Skylar? Will you sue?"

"Sue? Sue who?"

"Jonesy. Dr. MacBride."

"Is that what I'm supposed to do?" Carefully, Skylar asked, "Is that what you want me to do, Jon Than?"

Jon said, "Frankly, my bro, I don't give a damn."

Skylar got up and resumed packing. "When I give her back her key, I'll tell Mrs. Fitz she can keep my week's rent."

"Where are you going?" Jon asked.

"Paxton Landing, right now."

"Skylar, Dad asked me not to bother you with all this. You matriculating at Knightsbridge and all."

"No loss."

"He says this should be a happy time for you."

"Shoulda been."

"Anyway, you don't need to pack to come to Paxton Landing. I've got plenty of clothes."

"Yes, you have. I did notice that, Jon Than. 'Specially belts."

"Keep your room here. You need it. Or are you going somewhere else after Paxton Landing?"

"I'm goin' home."

"Why?"

"Emasculation. Jon Than, the threat, even the thought of emasculation can't make me happy."

Jon watched Skylar smoothing clothes in his suitcase. "You think I'm emasculated? You think we're all emasculated."

"No."

"Then what do you think?"

"I think I don't want to be emasculated. In any way. Surely not just for walkin' and talkin', bein', just as politelike as this particular boy can be. And that, Jon Than, is exactly as far as my thinking goes on emasculation."

After a long silence, after Skylar snapped the suitcase shut, Jon asked, "Skylar, I came by to ask: Is there any chance you know where, on God's earth, Ginny might be?"

Skylar picked up his suitcase. "I do have a thought on the topic. Yes, sir, I surely do."

At Paxton Landing, Lacey knew she was wandering senselessly around the house.

She was tired of the meetings going on continuously in the study with Wayne, Vance, the attorney, Randall Hastings, and his assistants coming and going, the public relations expert, Coyne Roberts. She had listened all she could, for now. It was just talk, talk, talk, when, in fact, no one knew anything.

Lacey wandered into Ginny's room. She had not been in the room since she had taken Ginny's personal telephone book.

Instantly, she noticed differences in the room.

Ginny's closet door was ajar. Could the police have left it that way?

Ginny's backpack was missing. So was the little radio she kept on her desk.

One of the bureau drawers was not shut completely.

Lacey went through the bureau drawers. Each looked less full than it ought. Underwear could have been missing, T-shirts, shorts, socks.

If Ginny had been here, changed clothes, packed other clothes, where was the pink party dress? Lacey could not find it in the closet, or in the clothes hamper.

However, on the floor of the closet was a space where a pair of sneakers might have been.

While looking for Ginny's personal telephone book, Lacey remembered finding eighty-nine dollars in cash in the middle drawer. She had left it there.

She opened the drawer.

The money was gone.

Ought Lacey tell the police Ginny somehow had sneaked into her room, packed clothes, her little radio, taken her money, and gone again? Where?

Where had Ginny gone?

No.

Instead, Lacey used the phone on Ginny's bedside table and had a quiet conversation with her husband in the study.

She said, "Wayne, I'm afraid this means Ginny has a plan to disappear somehow. . . ."

"It's for you, Skylar Whitfield." At the bottom of the stairs of the rooming house on Marly Street, Mrs. Fitz held out the telephone receiver. "At least I think it is. I'm not understanding the caller too well."

"Hello?"

"Hydy, Skylar. How're you doin'?"

"Ha, Dufus!"

Across the foyer, Mrs. Fitz was telling Jon and Alex her husband had been a saxophone player. Skylar heard her mention Benny Goodman.

"How are all those people up there in Yankeeland?"

"Don't ask."

"Calder?"

"Don't ask."

"She carries her nose so high, she prolly run herself into a tree."

"You're not far wrong, Dufus."

"And Ginny? Least she tried to be nice to me. You seen any sign of that blue Dodge Ram pickup truck your uncle Wayne said he was gonna buy me last June?"

"No, sir, I haven't." Upon returning to Tennessee, Dufus had told Skylar Wayne had said he would buy Dufus a blue Dodge Ram pickup truck. A new one. Dufus had been excited about it at first. When week after week went by and Dufus heard nothing about the truck, nothing at all from Wayne, he and Skylar had made a running joke out of the expected blue Dodge Ram pickup truck, as they worked the farm, worked on the car for the demolition derby. "Maybe I'll be able to explain that when I get home. Why are you calling, Dufus?"

"Skylar, you have any idea what we can do with twenty-eight thousand car dashboards?"

"You have twenty-eight thousand car dashboards?"

"Yes, sir. We do."

"Put them on twenty-eight thousand cars?"

"We don't have twenty-eight thousand cars, Skylar."

"Dufus, how come you have twenty-eight thousand dashboards?"

"They're in Jimmy Bob's eighteen-wheeler, is what the manifest says."

"You have Jimmy Bob's eighteen-wheeler?"

"Yes, sir, we do."

"Where? Why?"

"At the moment we've got it pretty well hidden in the quarry. Skylar, you have no idea how hard it is to hide an eighteen-wheeler until you try to hide one."

"I expect you're right, Dufus. But why do you have the eighteen-wheeler?"

"Well, Jimmy Bob, he was fixin' to leave the state in it, you see. That would have complicated matters considerably."

"That's his job, isn't it? To drive the truck long-haul?"

"It was. Jimmy Bob won't be able to hold any job for a while now, Skylar."

"Why not? Dufus, where is Jimmy Bob?"

"He's in a ditch just this side of the state line, Skylar. He's beat up pretty bad."

"Did he have an accident?"

"Lots of 'em. He kept runnin' into our fists and boots. Over and over again. We beat that boy up real good. Left him in a ditch. Took his eighteen-wheeler. You know, those things aren't so hell-fire hard to drive, although I do admit to grinding down some of the gears I didn't know the thing had."

"Dufus! Why did you all beat up Jimmy Bob?"

"Because this afternoon, before leavin' to pick up his loaded eighteen-wheeler at the truck terminal, Jimmy Bob beat the livin' daylights out of Tandy, Skylar. We didn't feel that was right."

"NO!"

"Yes. First we had to take her to the hospital. Then we had a pretty good time cotchin' up to Jimmy Bob. I figure he wasn't too surprised to see us all in his mirrors."

"How badly did he hurt Tandy?"

"Two black eyes, cut on her upper lip that needed

stitchin', cut on her forehead, a few broken ribs, a broken arm. She'll live. Don't bother tryin' to call her at the hospital, Skylar. With those stitches on her lip, she can't talk. Anyway, you'd just make her laugh, Skylar. You always have."

"That sombitch!"

"That's exactly what we thought! He's in much worse shape than she is, now that we stomped him like the snake he is. He's in no condition even to slither across the border. He'll be in the hospital a whole lot longer than Tandy will. Then maybe the jailhouse, once your daddy knows about it. We told the cops where to find him. But we didn't tell 'em where to find the eighteen-wheeler. You got any use for twenty-eight thousand dashboards, Skylar?"

"After dark, Dufus, bring the eighteen-wheeler back to the terminal. Just park it there. Be sure and wipe all your fingerprints off it, Dufus, outside and inside. And don't leave any cigarette packs or beer cans in it."

"Gotcha."

"And tell Tandy I'll be home sometime this week."

"True?"

"True."

"For good and all?"

"Yeah."

"Ha, Skylar!" Dufus laughed. "Those folks up there in Yankeeland didn't dig you any better than they did me!"

Chapter 21

The Oglethorps—Mr. and Mrs. Edward Nance as they now should have been referred to but generally were not, especially in Paxton—had talked about it and agreed it was best to try to keep to their routines as much as possible.

Edward Nance opened the French doors in the living room at six o'clock and Jilly scooted through onto the terrace in her wheelchair.

Then he made their drinks, picked up the plate of crackers and cheese from the kitchen table, and brought them to the terrace.

First he served his wife.

Then he sat in his usual chair on the terrace, next to the wicker, glass-topped table. He put the hors d'oeuvre plate on the table beside him.

There wasn't much they could do anyway.

The coroner had not yet released Louise's body.

Even though it was Labor Day, Edward had spent time that afternoon with a local funeral director. He had brought a dress Jilly had chosen from Louise's closet, chosen a coffin for the child. Of course the coffin would be closed. Part of the local cemetery was the Oglethorp family plot. He had arranged to have a grave dug.

They could not establish the timing of the memorial service or burial until they knew more from the police.

Edward asked, "Is there any news of the Whitfield girl? Is she still missing?"

"As far as I know. With Louise murdered, I expect Ginny is just a frightened child, hiding out somewhere. Do you think possibly she could have seen something, or know something? Maybe she thinks whoever murdered Louise wants to murder her, too. Maybe they both saw something, at the party or somewhere."

"No use in speculating." Edward took a sip of his gin and tonic. "I suppose the press will be on to this story tomorrow."

"I suppose." With red, puffy eyes, Jilly looked out to the river. She had been seeing that stretch of river all her life. Tonight she was not seeing it at all.

"If there's anything good about this situation," Edward said, "it's been that, thanks to the holiday, and to Lieutenant Hellman Forrest, I guess, we weren't hit by the press immediately. Given a little time to adjust."

Jilly said, "I'll never adjust."

"You want to name someone to speak for us?" Edward asked. "Or do you want me to do it?"

"Can you do it?"

"I can try. Whatever you think best. We haven't been married that long. But from being head basketball coach, I do have experience handling the press."

Edward started to put his glass on the table beside

him. He wanted another piece of cheese.

The coaster was not in its usual place. He leaned sideways to move the coaster nearer to him.

Under the coaster was a folded piece of paper.

After putting the coaster where he wanted it and setting his drink on it, he picked up the piece of paper.

While Jilly kept talking, Edward opened the paper. And read what was written on it.

Dear Mr. Edward Nance:

This is to inform you that I have Louise's diary. You didn't know Louise kept a diary? Too bad. Only I knew where she kept it.

In the diary Louise has written down exact descriptions of every time you have sexually abused her, including penetrating her, day or night, in the months since you married Mrs. Oglethorp.

Mrs. Oglethorp being in a wheelchair made things impossible for Louise. She did not want to or know how to tell her mother what you were doing to her. For the longest time she did not know what to do but grin and bear it. Grimace and bear it. Louise also put in her diary how really good you are to Mrs. Oglethorp. (Except you were screwing her 13-year-old daughter.)

And that you would say to Louise you were "just playing with her" and "teaching her things about sex she needed to know" and that it was "great that she had you to show her these things" and that "you loved her as much as her mother" and that all this must remain "a nice little secret" between you and Louise.

Louise asked you to stop, if you loved her, promise

never to do it again, and you'd say, "Oh, come on. We're just having fun. Aren't you having fun, Louise?"

You recognize your own words?

No. She was not "having fun."

Let me tell you, Mister—Louise didn't think there was anything "nice" about it. You kept her trapped for months. She really suffered, all thanks to you.

Well, I'm just waiting around until I catch one of these policewomen coming and going, which will probably be tomorrow, so I can show her the diary, give it to the police, as evidence.

Right now, I just want you to know you're not getting away with anything, bastard.

Virginia Whitfield

P.S. I also saw what happened in the woods late Saturday night. You were surprised Louise had a gun. You took it from her. She got shot in the face.

You want proof I saw it all?

I'm the one who moved Louise to the place under the big tree. I was trying to carry her to the house or someplace someone would find her. Didn't the fact that Louise's body had been moved puzzle you? It should have. Did you think Louise was able to crawl that far after you shot her?

On the terrace, Jilly was saying, "Really, I don't care. I just want to be completely isolated from the press. From everybody. I cannot make a statement. No matter how short, I couldn't get through it. In fact, I think I'll come to a point pretty soon at which I won't want to talk about this ever again. Even to you, Edward." She watched him fold a piece of paper and put it in his shirt pocket. "What's that?"

"A list," Edward Nance said. "Gardening tools I mean to get. I forgot I left it here."

Together Jilly and Edward sat at the dining-room table. They consumed their cold consommé, but when the maid served them the entrée of cold ham and pineapple, Jilly just looked at her plate and sighed.

"I don't seem to remember if Louise had a favorite flower," Jilly said. "Do you, Edward?"

"Carnations."

Jilly looked at her husband. "How do you know that?"

He shrugged. "She must have mentioned it to me sometime."

For a half hour the Nances sat at table, pretending to eat, pretending to converse.

Jilly had not slept at all Sunday night. She was numb with exhaustion and grief.

Edward's mind was awhirl. A diary? Goddamn it, a diary? That Louise was keeping a diary she had not mentioned to him. He had never thought of the possibility. He should have thought of it. As a group, thirteen-year-old girls typically keep diaries, don't they? Usually filled with boys' glances, daydreams about film stars, and their own sighs. And typically only their best friends know where the diary is kept. Agreeing never ever to read each other's diaries is a major pact between best friends at age thirteen, isn't it? Was Louise keeping this diary purposely as evidence against him? Of course it would be in Louise's own handwriting. He could deny everything in the diary, of course. He could say it was just the sexual fantasies of a schoolgirl regarding the man who had married her mother. Yes. While speaking to the police and press tomorrow, he would begin to allow all to infer that he suspected Louise had a schoolgirl crush on him.

That would be good. Nullify the diary. Before people knew of it.

Virginia Whitfield. Ginny.

Damned little brat.

Had she really seen what happened in the woods Saturday night?

Indeed, someone had moved the body.

Edward had worried about that—who? why?—since yesterday noon.

He had been able to think of no explanation. Except he figured that Ginny must have had something to do with it, when he learned she had disappeared.

Damned brat!

After the party at Paxton Landing Saturday night, after helping his wife into her bed, Edward had gone looking for Louise. He was ready to play.

In the short satin shift Louise had worn to the party, she stood in the moonlight on the lawn of Paxton Landing. At first he thought she was waiting for him.

Edward Nance just knew Louise enjoyed some of the things they did together. She had responded to him, sexually, sometimes.

Edward knew people said he had married Jilly for money.

That wasn't fair.

He had married out of love.

For Louise.

Had she seen him in the dark?

As he approached, Louise faded into the woods.

She and Ginny had made a game of leading him a merry chase through the woods along the river. Even when they played this game together in the daylight instead of after dark, he had never discovered where they hid. They would split up. They would throw stones behind him, or beside him, just to make a noise, give him a false sense of where they were. That much he knew. Sometimes they would appear to be on all sides of him at once.

He had enjoyed playing that game with the girls. It frustrated him, but it excited him, too.

Sooner or later he would be with Louise again. He would laugh and call her his "little wood nymph."

If Ginny had really seen what happened in the woods Saturday night, why hadn't she told the police?

Apparently it was Ginny's gun, a gun she had taken from her mother's bedside table, or so Lieutenant Forrest had told him. Ginny and Louise lost their tempers with each other, yelled at each other almost every day. Everyone saw it, heard it, knew it.

If she told such a story, it would not be believed.

Edward Nance was a respectable man. Louise's stepfather. He had offered to adopt her.

Right. Tomorrow when speaking sadly, solemnly of this tragedy, he must also feed in this long-standing, deep-seated rage Ginny had for Louise. And that everyone had witnessed it, time and again.

Why had Ginny left him that note?

Because Ginny knew she wouldn't be believed when she said she had witnessed the murder. She wanted him to know that with the diary—

"I'm going up to our room, Edward." Jilly backed her chair away from the table. "I just want to be alone awhile. But you will come up and help me in an hour or so?"

"Of course."

"You're looking particularly awful yourself," she said. "Even if we don't sleep, we need an early night. The doctor said bed rest is almost as good as sleep. Damned fool that he is."

Edward sat at the dining table listening to Jilly ascend in the elevator.

At the sideboard, he poured himself a double brandy. He swallowed it in one gulp.

Then he returned to the terrace.

It was dusk.

From stress, he supposed, from the belt of brandy on top of the gin, he suddenly felt a little woozy.

He focused his eyes on the river.

Something moving along the edge of the woods to his left caught his eye.

Odd clothes.

A bare-legged, bare-armed girl in a flouncy pink party dress, head down, was walking toward the river.

Under the girl's arm was a bright red book.

"Ginny?"

Without looking up, or changing her pace, the girl turned to her left, into the woods.

"Ginny!" he called. "Wait up!"

Edward walked rapidly along the terrace, down the steps to the lawn. On the lawn he broke into a trot until he reached the edge of the woods.

Once inside the woods, he called, "Ginny! I need to talk to you!"

Ahead of him, he saw just a flash of the pink dress.

Edward ran a few steps. By now, he knew these woods pretty well, but of course not as well as Ginny knew them. There was the main path along the river where local people walked and jogged. But there were many paths crisscrossing the woods. These secondary paths were never cleaned of stumps, fallen branches.

"Hey!" he yelled.

The girl did not look around, hurry her pace, or slow down.

In the last light of day, head down, red book under her arm, she walked along in her pink party dress, ducking under some fallen branches and easily stepping over rotting stumps.

Was he sure it was Ginny?

She seemed unreal.

"Ginny! Don't be afraid of me!"

Why didn't she look around? She must be hearing him.

Edward fell over a stump.

After dusting off his clothes, he ran a few more paces.

The girl seemed to keep the exact same distance between them without hurrying, without changing her pace.

On the river, an outboard motor–driven canoe also worked its way upstream.

"Ginny!"

Edward realized that for once, as he played this game in the woods, he was being led in a more or less straight line, upriver. He was about to come to Judge Ferris's property.

Could he make better time if he went toward the river and followed the clear path upstream?

No. He must not lose sight of the girl.

Against the evening sky he caught a glimpse of the top of the tower, the folly, on Judge Ferris's property.

Edward had never been led this far along the river. Usually the girls had run him in circles in the acres of woods between properties.

He came onto clear lawn.

The girl had already crossed the patch of lawn. She was walking into the woods near the tower.

Edward glanced at the back of Judge Ferris's house. "Ginny!" he hissed.

He could not see her.

Clearly she had been heading for the tower.

Slackening his pace, as if just out for an evening stroll, he crossed the lawn. He was aware he could be seen by Judge Ferris or someone else in his house.

He walked over rough ground to the base of the tower.

"Well, I'll be damned."

Edward stood over the hatch to the tower's cellar. He looked down the steep stone steps. Somewhere below a candle flickered.

So that was where the girls would hide out while they were playing hide-and-seek with him. No wonder he had never been able to find them. The little rats had a rathole to crawl into.

From the cellar came the sound of music, playing softly.

That must be why Ginny hadn't heard him. Besides the book she was carrying, she must also have been carrying a radio.

So she didn't know he had been following her.

She didn't know he was here.

He had her. Nothing to worry about. No more problems.

Stepping slowly, careful not to trip on the threshold, not to hit his head on the heavy metal hatch, Edward Nance went down the long, steep flight of stone steps into the folly's rock-walled cellar.

Softly, gently, he called, "Ginny?"

Above him, Ginny stepped out of the tower. She walked around the hatch she and Louise had kept well greased. Pushing, she slid the hatch closed tight.

Walking around the hatch again, she clasped its hasp.

Then she said, "Rot in hell."

Chapter 22

"Damn it, Skylar! Ginny's not here!" Beneath the folly on Judge Ferris's property, Jon leaned over the bulkhead hatch and examined the hasp with his fingers. Alex Broadbent beamed his flashlight on the hasp. "She couldn't be! The hatch is closed and hasped."

"I guess you're right, Jon Than." Skylar sighed. "I was pretty sure . . . I guess I was dead wrong. Sorry, you all."

"Now I'm more worried than ever," Jon muttered. "What could have happened to her?"

Alex ran the flashlight's beam up the outside wall of the stone tower. "Could she be inside the tower?"

Arriving at Paxton Landing not long after full dark, Skylar had led Jon and Alex to the river. From the dock, Skylar had stepped down into a canoe.

"We're going by water?" Alex had brought his flashlight from his car. "I'm still in my get-Skylar-out-of-jail clothes."

"It's the only way I know how to get where we're goin'," Skylar said.

With Alex sitting in the middle of the canoe, Skylar and Jon paddled upstream.

Just to make sure, Skylar, in the bow, paddled around the tiny island on which he and Ginny had had their picnic.

Jon said, "Skylar, you are not filling me with confidence. We're going in a circle."

"I know." In the rising moonlight, no one was visible on the island. Nothing like a boat touched the shore. "Just checkin'."

"Nothing like a moonlight cruise," Alex said. "Pity I didn't bring my mandolin."

"You mean Barry Mandolin?" Skylar asked.

Heading upstream again, Skylar said, "Ho! What's that?" He steered for a soft bulk bobbing in the moonlit river.

As the object came alongside the canoe, Alex grabbed it up. He dropped it between his shoes on the bottom of the canoe. He examined it in the light of his flashlight.

"A girl's pink party dress," he said.

"Ginny's," Jon said. "Oh, God."

"Relax," Alex said, "At least she's not in it."

When Skylar headed for the riverbank, Jon said, "Ferris's Folly? Skylar, you think that's where Ginny is?"

"Yes, sir. She showed me it Saturday. She and Louise had made sort of a clubhouse out of it. Out of the cellar. They had stocked it with food, blankets, candles, books."

"Damn!" Jon paddled harder. "Why didn't I think of that? I ran right by here yesterday. Twice."

"There's a path along the river, Skylar," Alex said. "We could have gotten here on foot."

"I didn't know that."

"Or by car," Alex added.

Inside the folly there was no sign of Ginny. Alex flashed his light up the steep steps to the top of the tower.

Jon ran up the steps.

Slowly, he walked down.

"No Ginny."

Outside the tower, they saw a flashlight approaching them through the woods.

"Rub-a-dub-dub!" a man's voice said. "Three men in a canoe."

"Judge Ferris?" Jon asked.

"If we ever need to invade anywhere again, I pray you three are not ordered to organize the excursion," Judge Ferris intoned. "Sitting on my porch in the dark, sipping my lonely cognac, I heard you on the river, saw your silhouettes, watched and heard you land. Is Ginny here?"

"No, sir," Skylar answered.

"As soon as I saw you approach I realized I should have thought that this would be a likely place for Ginny to hide, if hiding is what Ginny is doing. I have seen Ginny and Louise play around this old folly often."

"We all played here," Jon said. "As kids."

"So did I," the judge said. "As a kid."

"I completely forgot about it," Jon said.

"In fact, I saw Ginny and you here, Skylar, Saturday afternoon."

"I guess I was wrong," Skylar said. "About her bein' here. Her not bein' here does seem to make things worse, somehow. I was pretty sure . . ."

The judge beamed his flashlight on the cellar hatch. "Did you check down there?"

"It was closed when we got here, Judge," Jon said. "And hasped on the outside."

"Might look anyway." With his light, Alex headed for the bulkhead. "Maybe we can see if she's been here, might come back."

From the dark of the woods, a light voice said, "Don't open that hatch."

"Ginny?" Jon yelped.

"And Skylar was not wrong," the voice said. "This is where I've been."

Both lights were on Ginny as she stepped out of the woods.

Carrying a backpack, she wore a clean T-shirt, shorts, socks, sneakers.

"You fixin' to go somewhere?" Skylar asked.

"I was. Until you bozos showed up. Sorry, Judge. You're screwing up my plans."

"That's all right," the judge said, "whatever a bozo is."

"Ginny," Jon said. "You'd better start talking. What plans? What have you been up to? Why have you had us all worried sick?"

Ginny dropped her backpack on the hatch.

Elbows on drawn-up knees, chin in hands, Ginny sat on the hatch. "Turn off those lights, will you? I've got a headache."

The judge sat beside Ginny on the hatch. He turned off his flashlight. "We've been considerably worried about you, my dear."

"Talk." Jon's voice was almost threatening.

Ginny said, "Okay, Jonathan. Don't go all-over big brother on me."

More lightly, Jon said, "Shut up and talk, brat."

"Okay." Quickly, as if reciting, Ginny said, "Mr. Nance has been sexually abusing Louise since he married Mrs. Oglethorp. Louise never knew what to do about it."

She told them that during the summer Louise had been spending more and more time in the tower's "dungeon," even coming there after her mother had gone to bed, to sleep without fear of being assaulted by her stepfather. "Sometimes," Ginny said, "she was so sore from whatever he did to her I noticed she couldn't even run or swim. I kept asking her what was the matter with her.

"Finally, she began telling me all about it.

"It made me sick."

Alex lit a cigarette.

She told them how Mr. Nance had followed them through the woods, even in daylight, to find out where Louise was hiding from him. And how they'd confuse him, run him around the woods, and then disappear into the cellar of the tower.

"I wanted to beat him with a stick.

"Louise couldn't take any more. Besides being sore and worried and tired, it was making her really sick, sick to her stomach. She began throwing up every morning. Nerves, I guess. It was pitiful.

"Saturday night, while Mr. Nance was pushing Mrs. Oglethorp through the front door of their house in her wheelchair to put her in the van to drive her to the party at our house, he gave Louise a big smile and wink and said he'd see her after the party. I was there. I saw him do it. It was totally clear to both of us what he meant.

"Louise told me she couldn't take any more.

"So I got the gun Mother keeps in her bedside table and gave it to Louise.

"Our plan was for her just to frighten him with it. Threaten him. Show him she had a gun. Tell him if he didn't leave her alone, she really would shoot him.

"Later Saturday night, a while after the Nances left our house, I went looking for Louise. I headed here. I figured she would come here to spend the night.

"I tripped over her body in the woods. I fell. . . ."

"God," Jon said.

In the moonlight, Judge Ferris put his arm around Ginny's shoulders.

Ginny wept.

"The gun was there, beside her. I figured Mr. Nance had gotten the gun away from Louise and shot her in the face, or the gun just went off or something." She shivered under the judge's arm.

"I sat with her all night. Most of the night my mind was blank, I guess. Suddenly the sun was rising. I didn't know what to do. I was the one who had taken the gun and given it to Louise. After all the noise Louise and I had made, pretending to swear and cuss at each other, threaten each other, I realized people might actually think I shot her. Damn Louise Uglythorpe! I loved her!"

"I know," Judge Ferris said. "We all did."

"I needed to let people know it was Mr. Nance. . . . I had no idea how.

"Who'd believe a thirteen-year-old kid about such a thing? People might think I was blaming him because I was guilty of killing Louise. Mr. Nance had been a big-time basketball coach.

"I really did not know what I was doing.

"I carried her, and the gun, all the way through the woods. It took hours. I tried to be careful with her. Oh, I didn't want to hurt her, cut her legs, face, get her dirty!" Suddenly, Ginny buried her face in Judge Ferris's shirt. Loudly crying, she said, "Oh, God!"

"It's all right, child," the judge said. "Take your time."

Skylar looked at the moon.

In woods under other moons he had listened to other stories.

None had horrified him as much as this one.

"I didn't exactly know where I was going with her, what I was doing. I felt it was my fault. I had given her the gun. I had to disappear, go away. But I wanted someone to find Louise's body. The gun. I couldn't leave her in the woods. I guess I had some idea of connecting her death to Mr. Nance. I found myself with her under the big tree on the Oglethorps' lawn. I was so tired.

"Then I saw Mrs. Palmer, Dot Palmer, walking her dog. I knew she saw me. She called out my name.

"So I dropped the gun.

"I came here.

"Would you believe I slept?"

"It's all right," Alex said. "Ginny, it's okay."

After a while, Ginny continued.

She told them about leaving Mr. Nance the note telling him that Louise had left a diary detailing his abuse of her.

And that Ginny had seen him shoot Louise.

And she told them how, in her pink party dress, pretending not to hear him, notice him, she had led Edward Nance through the woods.

And with a lighted candle and a softly playing radio she had lured him into the tower's cellar, the "dungeon," and trapped him there.

"Edward Nance is in here?" Judge Ferris pointed between his legs to the metal hatch on which he sat. "In my great-grandfather's wine cellar?"

Ginny said, "To rot."

"That was your plan?" Jon asked.

The judge asked, "Do you suppose he's hearing all this?"

"No," Ginny said. "You can't hear a thing down there when this hatch is closed."

"Right," the judge said. "At one time the old place was fitted up as a bomb shelter."

"And we can't hear him." Ginny giggled through a nose filled from crying. "I bet he's down there hollering his leathery old basketball coach's lungs out."

"I do believe," Judge Ferris mused, "this is the first criminal case I literally have sat on."

"Ginny," Alex asked, "why did you do things this way? I don't understand. Sure, you may have been afraid you'd be accused—"

"There is no diary," Ginny said. "All I had to bait him with was his own words that Louise had only told me. The red book I carried was a novel Louise had left here.

"And I didn't actually see him murder Louise."

"I see," Alex said.

Ginny asked, "Isn't the fact that he followed me here after he read the note proof enough of his guilt? He was coming to kill me, too, because he thought I had a diary, and had seen him murder Louise."

"You took a great risk, my dear," the judge said. "It sounds to me, Ginny, that you haven't much faith in our judicial system."

"I don't." Ginny sat up. "Why should I? Look at all the trials, of the Menendez brothers, O. J. Simpson. . . . Lawyers deconstruct that which is evidentiary truth. . . ."

" 'Deconstruct'?" Alex said. "Where did you learn a word like that? A concept like that?"

"Mrs. Palmer." Ginny sniffled. "Dot Palmer. She's

a college teacher. She talks to us kids all the time."

"Oh, I'm sorry." Judge Ferris sighed mightily. "This makes me as sad as all the rest of this tragedy. That you feel that way—"

"Of course I do," Ginny said. "Don't we all? Isn't that why there is so much violence? Sorry, Judge, but who believes in courts? Mrs. Palmer says the concept of factual truth—"

"Never mind about Mrs. Dot Palmer," the judge said.

"If I had gone to the police, my family would have been put through hell for years," Ginny said. "Better I should do what I had to do, and just disappear."

The judge said, "Oh, Ginny."

"Were you really going to leave him here, Ginny?" Jon asked. "Let Edward Nance rot in your dungeon?"

Quickly, the judge said, "Don't answer that, Ginny."

After a moment, the judge stood up. "It's all right, Ginny. I think you'll find there will be plenty of evidence against Mr. Edward Nance impossible to deconstruct, as you put it."

"Sure," Ginny said. "What?"

"The coroner reports Louise's body shows much evidence of sexual abuse. And," the judge said, "Louise was seven weeks pregnant."

"Oh, God," Jon said.

"I believe there will be enough physical, scientific evidence against Mr. Edward Nance presented to whatever judge and jury to see that Edward Nance finishes rotting soon enough, one way or another."

"God!" Jon reached for the hasp. "Let him out! I'll strangle the bastard!"

"No!" Ginny said. "Don't open the hatch!"

"No, Jonathan," the judge said.

Skylar said, "Better to let the sombitch rot right where he is, Jon Than. Save all those judges and juries a lot of bother and expense. You haven't got any good wine stored down there right now, do you, Judge? Any you'd particularly miss?"

Alex said, "You know we have to let him out, Judge. Bring him to your house. Call the police."

"No, we don't." The judge turned his light on the hatch. "Looks a good hasp to me. I don't know anything about this particular matter. Do I, Ginny?"

"No, Judge."

"Jon?"

"No."

"Alex?"

"I guess you can't."

"Skylar?"

Skylar answered, "Then I don't either."

The judge said, "I guess I'll leave it to you, Alex, to call your friends on the police sometime during the night, or tomorrow morning if it would be more convenient for you, and tip them off as to where they can find Edward Nance? Of course, I expect you to call your newspaper first. . . ."

The judge added, "I trust each of you to do what is right."

The beam from his flashlight preceding him, the judge started back toward his house.

At the edge of the wood, he turned around. He raised his head to look at the top of the tower.

The rough, gray stone walls shone solid, strong in the moonlight.

"Well, well, well," the judge said. "Wouldn't my great-grandfather be pleased to know this stupid folly he built finally served a useful purpose. . . ."

Chapter 23

"What's this I see before me?" Jon asked. "What walks?"

Having left the canoe tied to the dock, Skylar and Jon were headed up the lawn toward the main house at Paxton Landing.

Not appearing to see them, Tom Palmer, nude, waddled by them and onto the dock.

Ginny with her backpack had decided to walk back from the folly with Alex Broadbent.

"Is Tom Palmer drunk again?" Skylar asked.

Going down the dock, Tom's ass shone alabaster white in the moonlight.

"I suspect he's still drunk from two nights ago," Jon said.

Tom fell or dove off the dock. He made a loud splash.

"You go ahead to the house," Jon said. "I'll take care of Tom, see that he doesn't drown this time. Tell Obadiah or Mrs. Watts we're hungry, will you? I'll be right there."

Skylar continued to the house.

Alex and Ginny had just arrived.

Skylar followed the noise to the study door.

In the study were his aunt Lacey, uncle Wayne, Vance Calder, Alex, Ginny, lots of people Skylar had never seen before. Ginny, still wearing her backpack, was the center of attention.

Everyone was talking at once.

Except Ginny.

Lacey was saying, "Judge Ferris called . . ."

Skylar turned around.

He almost bumped into Obadiah rushing out of his pantry.

"Hey, sir!" Skylar said. "Some of us are pretty hungry. If—"

"I'll take care of it," Obadiah said in his rapid English. But he continued hastening toward the noise in the study. "Ginny back? Ginny all right? A few minutes, please, sir—"

Smiling, enjoying the happy noises coming from the study, Skylar wandered around the living room.

He studied some of the paintings. He studied the wide, dark floorboards. He studied the exposed, hand-hewn ceiling beams.

This sure is one old house, he said to himself. Even older than ours. Driveway made out of boulders. Whoever heard of such an outlandish thing?

I still say a few goats, other animals, around might improve this old place.

Calder looked through the living-room door at Skylar.

"You still here?" she asked.

"Just leavin'," Skylar said. "Pretty soon."

"You needn't wait to be excused," she said.

She turned toward the study.

Having a few goats, and other animals, around here might improve some of the people who live here, too, Skylar said to himself.

Teach 'em a few manners, for one thing.

After a while, wondering what had delayed Jon, Skylar left the house and went back down the lawn toward the dock.

Jon, head and shoulders propped up on his elbows, was lying in the moonlight in the mud at the edge of the river.

Skylar asked, "What you doin' down there, Jon Than?"

Bending his knees, Skylar crouched over him.

Jon was breathing heavily. His stomach muscles were pumping up and down as if he had sprinted a mile.

His face and body were scarred with mud. There was even mud in his hair.

"You lost your shirt somewhere," Skylar said. "Jon Than, you happen to notice your shorts are down around your ankles?"

"Sombitch tried to rape me."

"What son of a bitch?"

"Skylar, don't go Yankee on me now! I said sombitch! I mean sombitch!"

"What sombitch?"

"Tom. Tom Palmer."

"That sombitch!" Skylar looked both ways along the river, up the lawn to the hedges defining the terraces. "You serious? Where is that sombitch?"

"Sombitch," Jon said. "He's long gone."

"Wha' happened?"

"On the dock, I took off my shirt and dove in after Tom. He was floating out, downstream, facedown. I tried to talk him in. He wasn't responding. I started to turn him over, lift his head out of the water, try get my arm around his chest. All of a sudden he came alive. Hittin' me in the head with both fists. Sombitch knocked me senseless.

"Next thing I knew I was here, facedown in the mud.

"Sombitch was kneeling over me, trying to put his thing in my asshole."

"Serious? That sombitch!" Skylar yelled. "He was tryin' to cornhole you, Jon Than?"

"That what you call it?"

"One word for it."

"You damned Southerners have a cute word for every goddamned thing under the sun, don't you?"

"Jon Than, you're takin' the Lord's name in vain again. Now, I've spoken to you about that—"

"Don't lecture me, you Southern . . . poltroon!"

"What's a poltroon, Jon Than?"

"Someone who comes from a place where they have cute words for every goddamned thing under the sun, no matter how repulsive it is! My God! Tom Palmer!" Jon put the back of his head onto the mud. He cupped one hand over his forehead. "I've known him all my life. He wanted to do that? What word did you use?"

"Cornhole."

"Cornhole. I don't get it."

"What did you do?"

"I broke his jaw."

"True?"

"I felt his bones crunch. I heard them crack. Definitely I broke his jaw. Big time." Jon's stomach muscles, now stretched out, were still pumping, but a little more easily. "It wasn't easy. He's a heavy guy."

"So he went away pretty well convinced you didn't

want to be cornholed, that right, Jon Than?"

"I don't understand. Sombitch knows I'm not interested in that sort of thing. . . ."

"Rape's about domination, Jon Than."

"Here comes that other Skylar," Jon said. "The one who knows shelves of books aren't really just thick wallpaper. You're such a phony, Skylar."

"Well, be that as it may, Jon Than, I'm up here, and you're down there."

Jon blinked into the moonlight. "You ever had the instinct to rape anybody, Skylar?"

"No, sir, I haven't. Not my style. Although once I did hit this damned big, arrogant, dump-ass stud upside the head with a shovel."

"You mean, you hit a horse, right? A real horse. A stallion. Not a man?"

"I think he was a horse, Jon Than. 'Least he had four legs. Is that a clue?"

Jon chuckled. "Sombitch." He sat up. He shook his head. "My head hurts."

"I 'spect it does," Skylar said. "When you shook it just then, I swear I heard the green water sloshin' around inside."

Jon said, "That sombitch is going to have a hard time explaining who broke his jaw and why. Not that he'll be able to talk for a few months."

Skylar grabbed Jon's right bicep. "Come on. Let me help you out of the mud, Jon Than. Let me raise you up!"

Standing, Jon said, "Wait a minute. My shorts are down."

"Raise up your shorts!" Skylar said. "Praise the Lord!"

"They're full of mud." Jon stepped out of his shorts and threw them into the river.

"Cast your shorts upon the waters! Praise the Lord!"

"Oh, shut up. Skylar, I'm dizzy."

Keeping him awake and moving, on the way up the lawn, Skylar told Jon about Tandy McJane and Jimmy Bob.

"Sombitch." Jon was staggering. "Good ol' Dufus. There's good blood in that boy."

"Yes, there sure is."

"Tom Palmer," Jon said.

Skylar said, "Sombitch."

Jon said, "No wonder that sombitch couldn't take my sister out without getting dead drunk."

Chapter 24

After Lacey got into bed and turned out the light, the door to her bedroom opened.

In his bathrobe, light from the sitting room behind him, Wayne entered her bedroom.

"Don't we need sleep?" Lacey asked.

Wayne turned on a reading lamp next to a small upholstered chair and sat down.

He said, "I'm afraid you have a decision to make."

Propped on the pillows on her bed, Lacey stared at her husband in the dim room.

Wayne said, "Whether you want to be a Calder or a Whitfield."

Lacey continued staring at him.

"Thing is," Wayne said, "I feel I've been a Calder long enough."

Lacey did not know whether to speak.

"Before you decide," Wayne said, "I have a couple of things to tell you.

"Dufus . . ."

Chapter 25

"How long you been gone?" Dan Whitfield asked his son.

"Seems like forever and two weeks." From the backseat of his parents' car, Skylar watched his bus pull out and gear south for Alabama.

"To us, too," his mother, Monica, said. "Although I don't know why. When you're here, we never know where you are."

"I know you want to get home," Dan said, "but I need to stop at the old Sinclair farm on the way, get some insurance papers signed. It shouldn't take long."

"Ah, yes," Skylar said. "Family named Repo, from Delaware, Tandy said. You met them yet?"

"Well," Dan said. "Repo, Inc. I don't know if that's their name."

"Haven't laid eyes on them," Monica said. "Or heard from anyone who has. They just arrived late last night. I'm bringing them a mince pie."

"Thought I smelled somethin' good," Skylar said.

"Suppose they'd miss a piece out of it?"

"Skylar, I am not going to greet our new neighbors with a pie you've already been into."

"Aw, shucks. Guess I'll have to make friends with 'em, to get myself a piece."

"You'll have your own pie, at home. If Dufus hasn't found it."

Skylar always felt like a little kid riding along in the backseat of his parents' sedan, with both of them in front.

But that's all right.

They're good folks.

Besides, when they were little kids, he and Tandy would ride along in the backseat, their bare legs twisted around each other, their faces angelic, in case his father happened to glance through the rearview mirror.

Skylar was disappointed Tandy hadn't come with his parents to pick him up from the Greendowns bus stop.

Perhaps she was disappointed he had spent those two nights in Washington, D.C., to tour the capital of the United States. On the telephone he had told her he never expected he would be that far north again.

On the bus ride south, Skylar had asked the driver to notify him when they were over the Mason-Dixon line. Only then did he take out his trumpet and play for the other passengers.

"Tell us about some of the folks you met, Skylar," Monica said.

"Oh, I met some real fine folks. A Mr. Alex Broadbent, who writes for a newspaper up there, and some of his artist and musical friends. A Judge Ferris. An ambassador . . ."

Over the phone, Skylar had already explained his

experience at Knightsbridge School of Music to his parents. He had told them little else.

"... the woman who ran my boardinghouse, a Mrs. Fitz ..."

"I'm not hearing you mention any of your cousins. What about Calder?"

"Well, Jon Than you know. Ginny is like me. A savage."

They were entering the long dirt driveway of the Sinclair farm.

"Hey!" Skylar sat up better to look through the backseat window. "That's Runaway! That's my horse! Who's that girl riding him?"

"It couldn't be," Monica said.

"It is. That's my dog Julep running along behind."

"You're right." Dan stopped the car. "What are they doing here?"

"Who's riding my horse?"

The girl approaching them on the galloping horse wore a riding helmet.

"Ginny?" Skylar said. "Is that Ginny? How can that be Ginny?"

"Ginny who?" Monica asked.

"Ginny Whitfield," Skylar said. "My cousin Ginny. Your niece. She can't be here!"

He got out of the car.

"Ha, Skylar!" Ginny drew up and stopped Runaway. "How're ya doin'?"

"Ginny! What are you doin' here?"

Runaway nuzzled Skylar. Julep was all over him with delight.

"I live here," Ginny said. "Arrived last night. Surprised?"

"I'll say."

"So am I," Ginny said.

Skylar introduced her to his parents. "You're Repo, Inc.?"

"What?" Ginny asked.

"You mean Wayne bought this place?" Dan asked the air. "Well, I'll be a hop-toad's hop."

"You all go ahead." Skylar climbed onto Runaway behind Ginny.

"My, my. Will wonders never cease?" Monica asked. "Wayne and Carolyn here. Why didn't they tell us?"

"Guess they wanted to surprise us," Dan said.

"Well, they surely have."

The car went up the driveway toward the house.

Ginny rode the horse at a walk along the side of the driveway.

"Suddenly the parental units told me to pack everything I wanted to keep," Ginny said. "That we were moving here. Calder decided to stay north. She's to move in with some friends in Boston."

"You had no idea you were coming here? I mean, beforehand?"

"None at all. Well, this is where I was headed, maybe, after I trapped Mr. Edward Nance in the dungeon. I wanted to see the yellow in your green hills, Skylar." She looked around. "It's gorgeous!"

"This is great!" From behind, Skylar hugged Ginny.

She giggled.

Then she asked, "Skylar, did you ever meet Mrs. Dot Palmer?"

"I know who she is."

"Was."

"What do you mean?"

"Mrs. Dot Palmer died in her sleep two nights ago. She took an overdose of drugs."

"Oh."

"You don't seem too upset. I guess you didn't know her."

"No. Not really."

A huge moving van was backed up to the front door of the house. Men were walking back and forth carrying furniture, boxes into the house.

Nearby was parked a blue Dodge Ram pickup truck.

On the porch, Monica and Dan, Lacey and Wayne were greeting each other happily.

"Oh, Monica," Lacey was saying. "No one has called me Carolyn in years! Please call me Lacey."

"How odd," Monica said, "in all these years we've never met. And here we all have grown children."

"Our fault, I'm afraid," Lacey said. "We were always caught up in things that didn't make any difference."

Skylar told his uncle and aunt how delighted he was to see them.

Both hugged Skylar.

"You sure know how to keep a secret, Uncle Wayne."

"Felt it was time I came home."

"You mean to make this your home?" Dan asked. "Your real home?"

"I sure do." Suddenly Wayne was sounding more Southern than Skylar had ever heard him.

"Ha, Skylar!" Dufus came out of the house.

"What're you doin' here?" Skylar asked.

"I rode Runaway over. Mr. Whitfield called the farm after your parents left."

"And that blue Dodge Ram truck?" asked Skylar.

"Mine!" yelled Dufus. "Mine! Mr. Wayne Whitfield bought it for me yesterday afternoon in Nashville and they all drove down in it. Only about a hundred miles on it."

"You've never even driven anything that new."

"No, I haven't. Isn't she beautiful?."

"She sure is. Now I'll bet you won't even ride in my ol' truck anymore."

"I apologized to Mr. Wayne for all the jokes we made about that truck. We thought he'd forgotten his promise."

"I didn't forget," Wayne said. "Just had other things on my mind."

Stiffly, Tandy McJane came around the corner of the house and up the steps to the front porch. "Ha, Skylar."

Skylar was going to give her a big, happy hug.

He stopped. He looked at her. Her two black eyes. The cut on her forehead. The stitches in her upper lip. Her left arm in a sling.

Skylar said, "Guess I can't leave you alone without you gettin' yourself in some kind of trouble."

"Am I real ugly?"

"Not to me." Skylar kissed Tandy on the only bit of her face that didn't look damaged. "Never have been. Never will be."

"Don't hug me. I've got a couple of cracked ribs, too."

"Sombitch. Where is Jimmy Bob now?"

"On a jail bunk, hurting bad, I understand," Tandy said. "No one in the county includin' his own family felt like puttin' up bail money for him."

"Awaiting trial," Dan said. "He'll be out of circulation a good long while."

"You got pictures of that mess?" The sight of Tandy's face nearly sickened Skylar. "What he did to her?"

"Yes," Dan said. "Plus medical reports. Jimmy Bob has made a statement. There's not much fight left in that boy."

"I just can't guess what happened to him." Tandy beamed at Dufus. "Apparently someone tried to hijack his truck. Then beat him up real bad. Left him in a ditch. But the truck turned up back at the terminal still loaded." She smiled as much as her stitched lip allowed. "You think that truck found its way back to the terminal all by itself?"

"Maybe," Dufus said. "Some of those new eighteen-wheelers have all kinds of fancy equipment on 'em."

Skylar said, "It's real bad luck beatin' up on a girl, I've heard tell."

Obadiah stood in the front door. He wore his white jacket.

"Why, Mr. Obadiah!" Skylar shook hands with him. "You came, too."

"Yes, sir, Mr. Skylar. I'm very pleased to see you."

"Guess you're goin' to have to learn to talk slower, Mr. Obadiah. There's nothin' wrong with us Southerners, 'cept we like to savor what we hear."

"Skylar?" Dufus asked. "You want to go ridin' with me in my new, blue, Dodge Ram pickup truck?"

"Does it hurt you to walk?" Skylar asked Tandy.

"Just a little."

"Want to walk home with me?"

"I walked here. And you'll need to walk Runaway home."

"Ginny can keep him, if she wants, for now," Skylar said.

"That's okay, Skylar. I've been ridin' Runaway the last hour. I'll come over to see you later. Maybe Dufus will give me a ride."

"I'll do that," Dufus said.

"Okay." Skylar took Tandy's hand. "Later, Dufus."

Skylar and Tandy went down the steps of the porch.

"Skylar?" Wayne followed them. "I need to talk with you a minute."

While Tandy gathered Runaway's reins in her right hand and waited, Wayne and Skylar walked at a different angle away from the house.

"Are you pleased we came here, Skylar?"

"Very. What's Repo, Inc?"

"A personal Delaware corporation I established years ago, and then never used much."

"What does 'Repo' mean?"

"Nothing. I'll have to go back and forth to Boston for a while, to make sure Vance closes down Calder Partners properly."

"You broke? It doesn't look it, your buyin' this place."

"Everything with the Calder name on it is lost. But it was Vance Calder who lost it all, not me."

"Uncle Wayne, you stole those gembobs yourself, didn't you?"

"Stole them? I guess you could say that. They were never in the safe, if that's what you mean. The poor guard sat in the study all night watching that little red light, thinking he was guarding jewelry that was upstairs with me. Under my pillow."

"How did you make the safe's little security light go off?"

"After dawn, after the guard had turned off the lights in the study, I turned off the circuit breaker for that room. So the guard thought someone had been in the safe. I guess he'll spend the rest of his life trying to figure that one out. It's okay. I made sure he got to keep his job."

"Is it going to do me any good to ask why you did it? You tellin' me all the Calder money is gone?"

"All gone. Some years ago I had well endowed Jonathan, Calder, and Ginny from my own earnings. Besides, they have other trusts from their grandparents." Wayne smiled. "I forgot to endow me. But I had given your aunt Lacey those gembobs, as you call them, out of my own earnings."

"She knows you took them?"

"Oh, yes. I told her."

"I'm surprised she came here."

"I am, too. A week ago, I didn't think she would. I gave her her choice. We've been through hard times lately, beginning with my heart attack. The collapse of Calder Partners. Calder. Ginny. That incident between Jonathan and Tom Palmer. I guess we both learned a lot the past few weeks, like what's important. The fact that we love each other suddenly became the most important thing."

"I'm glad. Now you're fixin' to tell me to shut up about all this, aren't you?"

"I wish you would."

Skylar laughed. "You got your wish."

"Sometime," Wayne said, "would you and Tandy take Lacey and me to the Holler? I'd like to see Mrs. Duffy again."

"Aunt Lacey know about all that?"

"I told her. I'd like to hear you play your trumpet sometime when you're not swinging from a balcony."

"You got it. I better go get Tandy out of the sun."

"See you," Wayne said.

"See you, Uncle."

Skylar and Tandy strolled toward Whitfield Farm. Runaway and Julep followed them.

"Skylar, seems to me you went north and brought half the North home with you."

Skylar peeled off his shirt. "Seems like." He laughed.

"Skylar, you all educated up now?"

"I suspect we both are a little better educated," Skylar said. "You and me."

"Sorry I told you you had to go north to that music school where they don't like music. That I was goin' to marry up with Jimmy Bob to get you gone for the sake of your education."

"Education costs."

"Your aunt and uncle movin' here mean we're goin' to be seein' more of that Jon thang?"

"He'll probably come home during his vacations from Harvard sometimes."

"Ain't we seen just about enough of that Jon thang?"

"He's a decent sort."

"Lordy, Lordy, Skylar! You're talkin' like a Yankee already! I'll have to break you of that real fast!"

On the porch, keeping out of the way of the movers, Lacey said, "Monica, I have so much to learn from you! What do we call African Americans in the South now?"

"Friends," Monica said. "Unless and until proven otherwise."